Henry Ridgely Evans

Spirit World Unmasked

Henry Ridgely Evans

Spirit World Unmasked

ISBN/EAN: 9783742862624

Manufactured in Europe, USA, Canada, Australia, Japa

Cover: Foto ©Andreas Hilbeck / pixelio.de

Manufactured and distributed by brebook publishing software
(www.brebook.com)

Henry Ridgely Evans

Spirit World Unmasked

THE
SPIRIT WORLD UNMASKED

ILLUSTRATED INVESTIGATIONS

INTO THE

Phenomena of Spiritualism and Theosophy

BY

HENRY RIDGELY EVANS

The first duty we owe to the world is Truth—all the Truth—
nothing but the Truth.—*"Ancient Wisdom."*

CHICAGO

LAIRD & LEE, PUBLISHERS

SPIRIT PHOTOGRAPH.
[Taken by the Author.]

TO MY WIFE

"It is no proof of wisdom to refuse to examine certain phenomena because we think it certain that they are impossible, as if our knowledge of the universe were already completed."

—*Prof. Lodge.*

"The most ardent Spiritist should welcome a searching inquiry into the potential faculties of spirits still in the flesh. Until we know more of *these*, those other phenomena to which he appeals must remain unintelligible because isolated, and are likely to be obstinately disbelieved because they are impossible to understand."—*F. W. H. Myers: "Proceedings of the Society for Psychical Research," Part XVIII, April, 1891.*

TABLE OF CONTENTS.

ILLUSTRATIONS.

PREFACE.

There are two great schools of thought in the world—materialistic and spiritualistic. With one, MATTER is all in all, the ultimate substratum; mind is merely the result of organized matter; everything is translated into terms of force, motion and the like. With the other, SPIRIT or mind is the ultimate substance—God; matter is the visible expression of this invisible and eternal Consciousness.

Materialism is a barren, dreary, comfortless belief, and, in the opinion of the author, is without philosophical foundation. This is an age of scientific materialism, although of late years that materialism has been rather on the wane among thinking men. In an age of such ultra materialism, therefore, it is not strange that there should come a great reaction on the part of spiritually minded people. This reaction takes the form of an increased vitality of dogmatic religion, or else culminates in the formation of Spiritualistic or Theosophic societies for the prosecution of occult phenomena. Spiritualists are now numbered by the million. Persons calling themselves mediums present certain phenomena, physical and psychical, and call public attention to them, as an evidence of life beyond the grave, and the possibility of spiritual communication between this world and the next.

The author has had sittings with many famous mediums of this country and Europe, but has seen little to convince him of the fact of spirit communication. The slate tests and so-called materializations have invariably been frauds. Some experiments along the line of automatic writing and psychometry, however, have demonstrated to the writer the truth of telepathy or thought-transference. The theory of telepathy explains many of the marvels ascribed to spirit intervention in things mundane.

In this work the author has endeavored to give an accurate account of the lives and adventures of celebrated mediums and occultists, which will prove of interest to the reader. The rise and growth of the Theosophical cult in this country and Europe is of historical interest. Theosophy pretends to a deeper metaphysics than Spiritualism, and numbers its adherents by the thousands; it is, therefore, intensely interesting to study it in its origin, its founder and its present leaders.

THE AUTHOR.

The Spirit World Unmasked

INTRODUCTORY ARGUMENT.

"If a man die, shall he live again?"—this is the question of the ages, the Sphinx riddle that Humanity has been trying to solve since time began. The great minds of antiquity, Socrates, Pythagoras, Plato and Aristotle were firm in their belief in the immortality of the soul. The writings of Plato are luminous on the subject. The Mysteries of Isis and Osiris, as practiced in Egypt, and those of Eleusis, in Greece, taught the doctrine of the immortality of the individual being. The Divine Master of Arcane knowledge, Christ, proclaimed the same. In latter times, we have had such metaphysical and scientific thinkers as Leibnitz, Fichte, Schelling, Hegel and Schleiermacher advocating individual existence beyond the grave.

It is a strange fact that the more materialistic the age, the deeper the interest in spiritual questions. The vitality and persistence of the belief in the reality of the spiritual world is evidence of that hunger for the ideal, for God, of which the Psalmist speaks—"As the hart panteth after water brooks so panteth my soul after Thee, O God!" Through the passing centuries, we have come into a larger, nobler conception of the Universal Life, and our relations to that Life, in which we live, move, and have our being. Granting the existence of an "Eternal and Infinite Spirit, the Intellectual Organizer of the mathematical laws which the physical forces obey," and conceiving ourselves as individualized points of life in the Greater Life, we are constrained to believe that we bear within us the undying spark of divinity and immortality. Evolution points to eternal life as the final goal of self-conscious spirit, else this mighty earth-travail, the long ages of struggle to produce man are utterly without meaning. Speaking of a future life, John Fiske, a leading American exponent of the doctrine of evolution, says ("The Destiny of Man"): "The doctrine of evolution does not allow us to take the atheistic view of the position of man. It is true that modern astronomy shows us giant balls of vapor condensing into fiery suns, cooling down into planets fit for the support of life, and at last growing cold and rigid in death, like the moon. And there are indications of a time when systems of dead planets shall fall in upon their central ember that was once a sun, and the whole lifeless mass, thus regaining heat, shall expand into a nebulous cloud like that with which we started, that the work of condensation and evolution may begin over again. These Titanic events must doubtless seem to our limited vision like an endless and aimless series of cosmical changes. From the first dawning of life we see all things working together toward one mighty goal, the evolution of the most exalted spiritual qualities which characterize Humanity. The body is cast aside and returns to the dust of which it was made. The earth, so marvelously wrought to man's uses, will also be cast aside. So small is the value which Nature sets upon the perishable forms of matter! The question, then, is reduced to this: Are man's highest spiritual qualities, into the production of which all this creative energy has gone, to disappear with the rest? Are we to regard the Creator's work as like that of a child, who builds houses out of blocks, just for the pleasure of knocking them down? For aught that science can tell us, it may be so, but I can see no good reason for believing any such thing."

A scientific demonstration of immortality is declared to be an impossibility. But why go to science for such a demonstration? The question belongs to the domain of philosophy and religion. Science deals with physical forces and their relations; collects and inventories facts. Its mission is not to establish a universal metaphysic of things; that is philosophy's prerogative. All occult thinkers declare that life is from within, out. In other words life, or a spiritual principle, precedes organization. Science proceeds to investigate the phenomena of the universe in the opposite way from without, in; and pronounces life to be "a fortuitous collocation of atoms." Still, science has been the torch-bearer of the ages and has stripped the fungi of superstition from the tree of life. It has revealed to us the great laws of nature, though it has not explained them. We know that light, heat, and electricity are modes of motion; more than that we know not. Science is largely responsible for the materialistic philosophy in vogue to-day—a philosophy that sees no reason in the universe. A powerful wave of spiritual thought has set in, as if to counteract the ultra rationalism of the age. In the vanguard of the new order of things are Spiritualism and Theosophy.

Spiritualism enters the list, and declares that the immortality of the soul is a demonstrable fact. It throws down the gauntlet of defiance to skepticism, saying: "Come, I will show you that there is an existence beyond the grave. Death is not a wall, but a door through which we pass into eternal life." Theosophy, too, has its occult phenomena to prove the indestructibility of soul-force. Both Spiritualism and Theosophy contain germs of truth, but both are tinctured with superstition. I purpose, if possible, to sift the wheat from the chaff. In investigating the phenomena of Spiritualism and Theosophy I will use the scientific as well as the philosophic method. Each will act, I hope, as corrective of the other.

PART FIRST.

SPIRITUALISM.

I. DIVISIONS OF THE SUBJECT.

Belief in the evocation of the spirits of the dead is as old as Humanity. At one period of the world's history it was called Thaumaturgy, at another Necromancy and Witchcraft, in these latter years, Spiritualism. It is new wine in old bottles. On March 31, 1847, at Hydeville, Wayne County, New York, occurred the celebrated "knockings," the beginning of modern Spiritualism. The mediums were two little girls, Kate and Margaretta Fox, whose fame spread over three continents. It is claimed by impartial investigators that the rappings produced in the presence of the Fox sisters were occasioned by natural means. Voluntary disjointings of the muscles of the knee, or to use a medical term "the repeated displacement of the tendon of the *peroneus longus* muscle in the sheath in which it slides behind the outer *malleolus*" will produce certain extraordinary sounds, particularly when the knee is brought in contact with a table or chair. Snapping the toes in rapid succession will cause similar noises. The above was the explanation given of the "Hydeville and Rochester Knockings", by Professors Flint, Lee and Coventry, of Buffalo, who subjected the Fox sisters to numerous examinations, and this explanation was confirmed many years after (in 1888) by the published confession of Mrs. Kane, *nee* Margaretta Fox. Spiritualism became the rage and professional mediums went about giving séances to large and interested audiences. This particular creed is still professed by a recognized semi-religious body in America and in Europe. The American mediums reaped a rich harvest in the Old World. The pioneer was Mrs. Hayden, a Boston medium, who went to England in 1852, and the table-turning mania spread like wild fire within a few months.

Broadly speaking, the phenomena of modern Spiritualism may be divided into two classes: (1) Physical, (2) Subjective. Of the first, the "Encyclopaedia Britannica", in its brief but able review of the subject, says: "Those which, if correctly observed and due neither to conscious or unconscious trickery nor to hallucination on the part of the observers, exhibit a force hitherto unknown to science, acting in the physical world otherwise than through the brain or muscles of the medium." The earliest of these phenomena were the mysterious rappings and movements of furniture without apparent physical cause. Following these came the ringing of bells, playing on musical instruments, strange lights seen hovering about the séance-room, materializations of hands, faces and forms, "direct writing and drawing" declared to be done without human intervention, spirit photography, levitation, unfastening of ropes and bandages, elongation of the medium's body, handling fire with impunity, etc.

Of the second class, or Subjective Phenomena, we have "table-tilting and turning with contact; writing, drawing, etc., by means of the medium's hand; entrancement, trance-speaking, and impersonation by the medium of deceased persons, seeing spirits and visions and hearing phantom voices."

From a general scientific point of view there are three ways of accounting for the physical phenomena of spiritualism: (1) Hallucination on the part of the observers; (2) Conjuring; (3) A force latent in the human personality capable of moving heavy objects without muscular contact, and of causing "Percussive Sounds" on table-tops, and raps upon walls and floors.

Hallucination has unquestionably played a part in the séance-room, but here again the statement of the "En-

cyclopaedia Britannica" is worthy of consideration:
"Sensory hallucination of several persons together who
are not in a hypnotic state is a rare phenomenon, and
therefore not a probable explanation." In my opinion,
conjuring will account for seven-eighths of the so-
called phenomena of professional mediums. For the
balance of one-eighth, neither hallucination nor legerdemain are satisfactory explanation. Hundreds of credible
witnesses have borne testimony to the fact of table-
turning and tilting and the movements of heavy objects
without muscular contact. That such a force exists is
now beyond cavil, call it what you will, magnetic, nervous, or psychic. Count Agenor de Gasparin, in 1854,
conducted a series of elaborate experiments in table-
turning and tilting, in the presence of his family and a
number of skeptical witnesses, and was highly successful. The experiments were made in the full light of day.
The members of the circle joined hands and concen-
trated their minds upon the object to be moved. The
Count published a work on the subject "Des Tables Tournantes," in which he stated that the movements of the
table were due to a mental or nervous force emanating
from the human personality. This psychic energy has
been investigated by Professor Crookes and Professor

Lodge, of London, and by Doctor Elliott Coues, of Washington, D. C., who calls it "Telekinesis." The existence of this force sufficiently explains such phenomena of the séance-room as are not attributable to hallucination and conjuring, thus removing the necessity for the hypothesis of spirit intervention. In explanation of table-turning by "contact," I quote what J. N. Maskelyne says in "The Supernatural":

"Faraday proved to a demonstration that table-turning was simply the result of an unconscious muscular action on the part of the sitters. He constructed a little apparatus to be placed beneath the hands of those pressing upon the table, which had a pointer to indicate any pressure to one side or the other. After a time, of course, the arms of the sitters become tired and they unconsciously press more or less to the right or left. In Faraday's experiments, it always proved that this pressure was exerted in the direction in which the table was expected to move, and the tell-tale pointer showed it at once. There, then, we have the explanation: expectancy and unconscious muscular action."

II. SUBJECTIVE PHENOMENA.

1. Telepathy.

The subjective phenomena of Spiritualism—trance speaking, automatic writing, etc.,—have engaged the attention of some of the best scientific minds of Europe and America, as studies of abnormal or supernormal psychological conditions.

If there are any facts to sustain the spiritual hypothesis, these facts exist in subjective manifestations. The following statement will be conceded by any impartial investigator: A medium, or psychic, in a state of partial or complete hypnosis frequently gives information transcending his conscious knowledge of a subject. There can be but two hypotheses for the phenomena—(1) The intelligence exhibited by the medium is "ultra-mundane," in other words, is the effect of spirit control, or, (2) it is the result of the conscious or unconscious exercise of psychic powers on the part of the medium.

It is well known that persons under hypnotic influence exhibit remarkable intelligence, notwithstanding the fact that the ordinary consciousness is held in abeyance. The extraordinary results obtained by hypnotizers point to another phase of consciousness, which is none other than the subjective or "subliminal" self. Mediums sometimes induce hypnosis by self-suggestion, and while in that state, the subconscious mind is in a highly receptive and exalted condition. Mental suggestions or concepts pass from the mind of the sitter consciously or unconsciously to the mind of the medium, and are given back in the form of communications from the invisible world, ostensibly through spirit control. It is not absolutely necessary that the medium be in the hypnotic condition to obtain information, but the hypnotic state seems to be productive ol the best results. The medium is usually honest in his belief in the reality of such ultra-mundane control, but he is ignorant of the true psychology of the case—thought transference.

The English Society for Psychical Research and its American branch have of late years popularized "telepathy", or thought transference. A series of elaborate investigations were made by Messrs. Edmund Gurney, F. W. H. Myers, and Frank Podmore, accounts of which are contained in the proceedings of the Society. Among the European investigators may be mentioned Messrs. Janet and Gibert, Richet, Gibotteau, and

Schrenck-Notzing. Podmore has lately summarized the results of these studies in an interesting volume, "Apparitions and Thought-transference, an Examination of the Evidence for Telepathy." Thought Transference or Telepathy (from *tele*—at a distance, and *pathos*—feeling) he describes as "a communication between mind and mind other than through the known channels of the senses." A mass of evidence is adduced to prove the possibility of this communication. In summing up his book he says: "The experimental evidence has shown that a simple sensation or idea may be transferred from one mind to another, and that this transference may take place alike in the normal state and in the hypnotic trance.

* * The personal influence of the operator in hypnotism may perhaps be regarded as a proof presumptive of telepathy." The experiments show that mental concepts or ideas may be transferred to a distance.

Podmore advances the following theory in explanation of the phenomena of telepathy:

"If we leave fluids and radiant nerve-energy on one side, we find practically only one mode suggested for the telepathic transference—viz., that the physical changes which are the accompaniments of thought or sensation in the agent are transmitted from the brain as undulations in the intervening medium, and thus excite corresponding changes in some other brain, without any other portion of the organism being necessarily implicated in the transmission. This hypothesis has found its most philosophical champion in Dr. Ochorowicz, who has devoted several chapters of his book "De la Suggestion mentale," to the discussion of the various theories on the subject. He begins by recalling the reciprocal convertibility of all physical forces with which we are acquainted, and especially draws attention to what he calls the law of reversibility, a law which he illustrates by a description of the photophone. The photophone is an instrument in which a mirror is made to vibrate to the human voice. The mirror reflects a ray of light, which, vibrating in its turn, falls upon a plate of selenium, modifying its electric conductivity. The intermittent current so produced is transmitted through a telephone, and the original articulate sound is reproduced. Now in hypnotized subjects—and M. Ochorowicz does not in this connection treat of thought-transference between persons in the normal state—the equilibrium of the nervous system, he sees reason to believe, is profoundly affected. The nerve-energy liberated in this state, he points out, 'cannot pass beyond' the subject's brain 'without being transformed. Nevertheless, like any other force, it cannot remain isolated; like any other force it escapes, but in disguise. Orthodox science allows it only one way out, the motor nerves. These are the holes in the dark lantern through which the rays of light escape.   *   *   * Thought remains in the brain, just as the chemical energy of the galvanic battery remains in the cells, but each is represented outside by its correlative energy, which in the case of the battery is called the electric current, but for which in the other we have as yet no name. In any case there is some correlative energy—for the currents of the motor nerves do not and cannot constitute the only dynamic equivalent of cerebral energy—to represent all the complex movements of the cerebral mechanism.' "

The above hypothesis may, or may not, afford a clue to the mysterious phenomena of telepathy, but it will doubtless satisfy to some extent those thinkers who demand physical explanations of the known and unknown laws of the universe. The president of the Society for Psychical Research (1894,) A. J. Balfour, in an address on the relation of the work of the Society to the general course of modern scientific investigation, is more cautious than the writers already quoted. He says:

"Is this telepathic action an ordinary case of action from a center of disturbance? Is it equally diffused in all directions? Is it like the light of a candle or the light of the sun which radiates equally into space in every direction at the same time? If it is, it must obey the law—at least, we should expect it to obey the law—of all other forces which so act through a non-absorbing medium, and its effects must diminish inversely as the square of the distance. It must, so to speak, get beaten out thinner and thinner the further it gets removed from its original source. But is this so? Is it even credible that the mere thoughts, or, if you please, the neural changes corresponding to these thoughts, of any individual could have in them the energy to produce sensible effects equally in all directions, for distances which do not, as far as our investigations go, appear to have any necessary limit? It is, I think, incredible; and in any case there is no evidence whatever that this equal diffusion actually takes place. The will power, whenever will is used, or the thoughts, in cases where will is not used, have an effect, as a rule, only upon one or two individuals at most. There is no appearance of general diffusion. There is no indication of any disturbance equal at equal distances from its origin and radiating from it alike in every direction.

"But if we are to reject this idea, which is the first which ordinary analogies would suggest, what are we to put in its place? Are we to suppose that there is some means by which telepathic energy can be directed through space from the agent to the patient, from the man who influences to the man who is influenced? If we are to believe this, as apparently we must, we are face to face not only with a fact extraordinary in itself, but with a kind of fact which does not fit in with anything we know at present in the region either of physics or of physiology. It is true, no doubt, that we do know plenty of cases where energy is directed along a given line, like water in a·pipe, or like electrical energy along the course of a wire. But then in such cases there is always some material guide existing between the two termini, between the place from which the energy comes and the place to which the energy goes. Is there any such material guide in the case of telepathy? It seems absolutely impossible. There is no sign of it. We can not even form to ourselves any notion of its character, and yet, if we are to take what appears to be the obvious lesson of the observed facts, we are forced to the conclusion that in some shape or other it exists."

Telepathy once conceded, we have a satisfactory explanation of that class of cases in modern Spiritualism on the subjective side of the question. There is no need of the hypothesis of "disembodied spirits".

Some years ago, I instituted a series of experiments with a number of celebrated spirit mediums in the line of thought transference, and was eminently successful in obtaining satisfactory results, especially with Miss Maggie Gaule, of Baltimore, one of the most famous of the latter day psychics.

Case A.

About three years prior to my sitting with Miss Gaule, a relative by marriage died of cancer of the throat at the Garfield Hospital, Washington, D. C. He was a retired army officer, with the brevet of General, and lived part of the time at Chambersburg, Penn., and the rest of the time at the National Capital. He led a very quiet and unassuming life, and outside of army circles knew but few people. He was a magnificent specimen of physical manhood, six feet tall, with splendid chest and arms. His hair and beard were of a reddish color. His usual street dress was a sort of compromise with an army un-dress uniform, military cut frock-coat, frogged and braided top-coat, and a Sherman hat. Without these ac-cessories, anyone would have recognized the military man in his walk and bearing. He and his wife thought a great deal of my mother, and frequently stopped me on the street to inquire, "How is Mary?" I went to Miss Gaule's house with the thought of General M— fixed in my mind and the circumstances surrounding his decease. The medium greeted me in a cordial manner. I sat at one end of the room in the shadow, and she near the window in a large armchair. "You wish for messages from the dead," she remarked abruptly. "One moment, let me think." She sank back in the chair, closed her eyes, and remained in deep thought for a minute or so, occasionally passing her hand across her forehead. "I see," she said, "standing behind you, a tall, large man with reddish hair and beard. He is garbed in the uniform of an officer—I do not know whether of the army or navy. He points to his throat. Says he died of a throat trouble. He looks at you and calls "Mary,—how is Mary?" "What is his name?" I inquired, fixing my mind on the words David M—. "I will ask", replied the medium. There was a long pause. "He speaks so faintly I can scarcely hear him. The first letter begins with D, and then comes a— I can't get it. I can't hear it." With that she opened her eyes.

The surprising feature about the above case was the

alleged spirit communication, "Mary—how is Mary?"
I did not have this in my mind at the time; in fact I had
completely forgotten this form of salutation on the part
of Gen. M—, when we had met in the old days. It is
just this sort of thing that makes spirit-converts.

However, the cases of unconscious telepathy cited in
the "Reports of the Society for Psychical Research," are
sufficient, I think, to prove the existence of this phase
of the phenomena.

T. J. Hudson, in his work entitled "A scientific demonstration of the future life", says: *   *   "When a
psychic transmits a message to his client containing information which is in his (the psychic's) possession, it
can not reasonably be attributed to the agency of disembodied spirits.   *   *   When the message contains facts known to some one in his immediate presence
and with whom he is *en rapport*, the agency of spirits of
the dead cannot be presumed. Every investigator will
doubtless admit that sub-conscious memory may enter as
a factor in the case, and that the sub-conscious intelligence—or, to use the favorite terminology employed by
Mr. Myers to designate the subjective mind, the
'subliminal consciousness'—of the psychic or that of his

client may retain and use facts which the conscious, or objective mind may have entirely forgotten."

But suppose the medium relates facts that were never in the possession of the sitter, what are we to say then? Considerable controversy has been waged over this question, and the hypothesis of telepathy is scouted. Minot J. Savage has come to the conclusion that such cases stretch the telepathic theory too far; there can be but one plausible explanation—a communication from a disembodied spirit, operating through the mind of the medium. For the sake of lucidity, let us take an example: A has a relative B who dies in a foreign land under peculiar circumstances, *unknown to A*. A attends a s ance of a psychic, C, and the latter relates the circumstances of B's death. A afterwards investigates the statements of the medium, and finds them correct. Can telepathy account for C's knowledge? I think it can. The telepathic communication was recorded in A's sub-conscious mind, he being *en rapport* with B. A unconsciously yields the points recorded in his sub-conscious mind to the psychic, C, who by reason of his peculiar powers raises them to the level of conscious thought, and gives them back in the form of a message from the dead.

Case B.

On another occasion, I went with my friend Mr. S. C., of Virginia, to visit Miss Gaule. Mr. S. C. had a young son who had recently passed the examination for admission to the U. S. Naval Academy, and the boy had accompanied his father to Baltimore to interview the military tailors on the subject of uniforms, etc. Miss Gaule in her semi-trance state made the following statement: "I see a young man busy with books and papers. He has successfully passed an examination, and says something about a uniform. Perhaps he is going to a military college."

Here again we have excellent evidence of the proof of telepathy.

The spelling of names is one of the surprising things in these experiments. On one occasion my wife had a sitting with Miss Gaule, and the psychic correctly spelled out the names of Mrs. Evans' brothers—John, Robert, and Dudley, the latter a family name and rather unusual, and described the family as living in the West.

The following example of Telepathy occurred between the writer and a younger brother.

Case C.

In the fall of 1890, I was travelling from Washington to Baltimore, by the B. & P. R. R. As the train approached Jackson Grove, a campmeeting ground, deserted at that time of the year, the engine whistle blew vigorously and the bell was rung continuously, which was something unusual, as the cars ordinarily did not stop at this isolated station, but whirled past. Then the engine slowed down and the train came to a standstill.

"What is the matter?" exclaimed the passengers.

"My God, look there!" shouted an excited passenger, leaning out of the coach window, and pointing to the dilapidated platform of the station. I looked out and beheld a decapitated human head, standing almost upright in a pool of blood. With the other male passengers I rushed out of the car. The head was that of an old man with very white hair and beard. We found the body down an embankment at some little distance from the place of the accident. The deceased was recognized as the owner of the Grove, a farmer living in the vicinity. According to the statement of the engineer, the old man was walking on the track; the warning signals were given, but proved of no avail. Being somewhat deaf, he did not realize his danger. He attempted to step off the track, but the brass railing that runs along the side of the locomotive decapitated him like the knife of a guillotine.

When I reached Baltimore about 7 o'clock, P. M., I hurried down to the office of the "Baltimore News" and wrote out an account of the tragic affair. My work at the office kept me until a late hour of the night, and I went home to bed at about 1 o'clock, A. M. My brother, who slept in an adjoining room, had retired to bed and the door between our apartments was closed. The next morning, Sunday, I rose at 9 o'clock, and went down to breakfast. The family had assembled, and I was just in time to hear my brother relate the following: "I had a most peculiar dream last night. I thought I was on my way to Mt. Washington (he was in the habit of making frequent visits to this suburb of Baltimore on the Northern Central R. R.) We ran down an old man and decapitated him. I was looking out of the window and saw the head standing in a pool of blood. The hair and beard were snow white. We found the body not far off, and it proved to be a farmer residing in the neighborhood of Mt. Washington."

"You will find the counterpart of that dream in the morning paper", I remarked seriously. "I reported the accident." My father called for the paper, and proceeded to hunt its columns for the item, saying, "You undoubtedly transferred the impression to your brother."

Case D.

This is another striking evidence of telepathic communication, in which I was one of the agents. L— was a reporter on a Baltimore paper, and his apartments were the rendezvous of a coterie of Bohemian actors, journalists, and *littcrati*, among whom was X—, a student at the Johns-Hopkins University, and a poet of rare excellence. Poets have a proverbial reputation for being eccentric in personal appearance; in X this eccentricity took the form of an unclipped beard that stood out in all directions, giving him a savage, anarchistic look. He vowed never under any circumstances to shave or cut this hirsute appendage.

L— came to me one day, and laughingly remarked: "I am being tortured by a mental obsession. X's beard annoys me; haunts my waking and sleeping hours. I must do something about it. Listen! He is coming down to my rooms, Saturday evening, to do some literary work, and spend the night with me. We shall have supper together, and I want you to be present. Now I propose that we drug his coffee with some harmless soporific, and when he is sound asleep, tie him, and shave off his beard. Will you help me? I can provide you with a lounge to sleep on, but you must promise not to go to sleep until after the tragedy."

I agreed to assist him in his practical joke, and we parted, solemnly vowing that our project should be kept secret.

This was on Tuesday, and no communication was had with X, until Saturday morning, when L— and I met him on Charles street.

"Don't forget to-night," exclaimed L— "I have invited E to join us in our Epicurean feast."

"I will be there," said X. "By the way, let me relate a curious dream I had last night. I dreamt I came down to your rooms, and had supper. E— was present. You fellows gave me something to drink which contained a drug, and I fell asleep on the bed. After that you tied my hands, and shaved off my beard. When I awoke I was terribly mad. I burst the cords that fastened my wrists together, and springing to my feet, cut L— severely with the razor."

"That settles the matter", said L—, "his beard is safe from me". When we told X of our conspiracy to relieve him of his poetic hirsute appendage, he evinced the greatest astonishment. As will be seen, every particular of the practical joke had been transferred to his mind, the drugging of the coffee, the tying, and the shaving.

Telepathy is a logical explanation of many of the

ghostly visitations of which the Society for Psychical Research has collected such a mass of data. For example: A dies, let us say in India and B, a near relative or friend, residing in England, sees a vision of A in a dream or in the waking state. A clasps his hands, and seems to utter the words, "I am dying". When the news comes of A's death, the time of the occurrence coincides with the seeing of the vision. The spiritualist's theory is that the ghost of A was an actual entity. One of the difficulties in the way of such an hypothesis is the clothing of the deceased—*can that, too, be disembodied?* Thought transference (conscious or unconscious), I think, is the only rational explanation of such phantasms. The vision seen by the percipient is not an objective but a subjective thing—a hallucination produced by the unknown force called telepathy. The vision need not coincide exactly with the date of the death of the transmitter but may make its appearance years afterwards, remaining latent in the subjective mind of the percipient. It may, as is frequently the case, be revealed by a medium in a séance. Many thoughtful writers combat the telepathic explanation of phantasms of the dead, claiming that when such are seen long after the death of persons, they afford indubitable evidence of the reality of spirit visitation. The reader is referred to the proceedings of the Society for Psychical Research for a detailed discussion of the *pros* and *cons* of this most interesting subject.

Many of the so-called materializations of the séance-room may be accounted for by hallucinations superinduced by telepathic suggestions from the mind of the medium or sitters. But, in my opinion, the greater number of these manifestations of spirit power are the result of trickery pure and simple—theatrical beards and wigs, muslin and gossamer robes, etc., being the paraphernalia used to impersonate the shades of the departed, the imaginations of the sitters doing the rest.

2. Table-Tilting—Muscle Reading.

In regard to Table-Tilting with contact, I have given Faraday's conclusions on the subject,—unconscious muscular action on the part of the sitter or sitters. In the case of Automatic Writing (particularly with the planchette), unconscious muscular action is the proper explanation for the movements of the apparatus. "Professor Augusto Tamburini, of Italy, author of 'Spiritismo e Telepatia', a cautious investigator of psychical problems," says a reviewer in the Proceedings of the Society for Psychical Research (Volume IX, p. 226), "accepts the verdict of all competent observers that imposture is inadmissible as a general explanation, and endorses the view that the muscular action which causes the movements of the table or the pencil is produced by the subliminal consciousness. He explains the definite and varying characters of the supposed authors of the messages as the result of self-suggestion. As by hypnotic or post-hypnotic suggestion a subject may be made to think he is Napoleon or a chimney sweep, so, by self-suggestion, the subliminal consciousness may be made to think that he is X and Y, and to tilt or wrap messages in the character of X and Y."

Professor Tamburini's explanation fails to account for the innumerable well authenticated cases where facts are obtained not within the conscious knowledge of the planchette writer or table-tilter. If telepathy does not enter into these cases, what does?

There are many exhibitions, of thought transference by public psychics, that are thought transference in name only. One must be on one's guard against these pretenders to occult powers. I refer to men like our late compatriot, Washington Irving Bishop—"muscle-reader" *par excellence* whose fame extended throughout the civilized world.

Muscle-Reading is performed in the following manner: Let us take, for example, the reading of the figures on a bank-note. The subject gazes intently at the figures on a note, and fixes them in his mind. The muscle-reader, blindfolded or not, takes a crayon in his right hand, and lightly clasps the hand or wrist of the subject with his left. He then writes on a blackboard the correct figures on the note. This is one of the most difficult feats in the repertoire of the muscle-reader, and was excelled in by Bishop and Stuart Cumberland. Charles Gatchell, an authority on the subject, says that the above named men were the only muscle-readers who have ever accomplished the feat. Geometrical designs can also be reproduced on a blackboard. The finding of objects hidden in an adjoining room, or upon the person of a spectator in a public hall, or at a distance, are also accomplished by skillful muscle readers, either by clasping the hand of the subject, or one end of a short wire held by him. Says Gatchell, in the *"Forum"* for April, 1891: "Success in muscle-reading depends upon the powers of the principal and upon the susceptibility of the subject. The latter must be capable of mental concentration; he must exert no muscular self-control; he must obey his every impulse. Under these conditions, the phenomena are in accordance with known laws of physiology. On the part of the principal, muscle-reading consists of an acute perception of the slight action of another's muscles. On the part of the subject, it involves a nervous impulse, accompanied by muscular action. The mind of the subject is in a state of tension or expectancy. A sudden release from this state excites, momentarily, an increased activity in the cells of the cerebral cortex. Since the ideational centres, as is usually held, correspond to the motor centres, the nervous action causes a motor impulse to be transmitted to the muscles. * * In making his way to the location of a hidden object, the subject usually does not lead the muscle-reader, but the muscle-reader leads the subject. That is to say, so long as the muscle-reader moves in the right direction, the subject gives no indication, but passively moves with him. The muscle-reader perceives nothing unusual. But, the subject's mind being intently fixed on a certain course, the instant that the muscle-reader deviates from that course there is a slight, involuntary tremor, or muscular thrill, on the part of the subject, due to the sudden interruption of his previous state of mental tension. The muscle-reader, almost unconsciously, takes note of the delicate signal, and alters his course to the proper one, again leading his willing subject. In a word, he follows the line of the least resistance. In other cases the conditions are reversed; the subject unwittingly leads the principal.

"The discovery of a bank-note number requires a slightly different explanation. The conditions are these: The subject is intently thinking of a certain figure. His mind is in a state of expectant attention. He is waiting for but one thing in the world to happen—for another to give audible expression to the name of that which he has in mind. The instant that the conditions are fulfilled, the mind of the subject is released from its state of tension, and the accompanying nervous action causes a slight muscular tremor, which is perceived by the acute senses of the muscle-reader. This explanation applies, also, to the pointing out of one pin among many, or of a letter or a figure on a chart. The conditions involved in the tracing of a figure on a blackboard or other surface are of a like order, although this is a severer test of a muscle-reader's powers. So long as the muscle-reader moves the crayon in the right direction, he is permitted to do so; but when he deviates from the proper course, the subject, whose hand or wrist he clasps, involuntarily indicates the fact by the usual slight muscular tremor. This, of course, is done involuntarily; but if he is fulfilling the conditions demanded of all subjects, absolute concentration of attention and absence of muscular control—he unconsciously obeys his impulse. A billiard player does the same when he follows the driven ball with his cue, as if by sheer force of will he could induce it to alter its course. The ivory is uninfluenced; the human ball obeys."

1. Psychography, or Slate-Writing.

One of the most interesting phases of modern mediumship, on the physical side, is psychography, or slate-
writing. After an investigation extending over ten years,
I am of the opinion that the majority of slate-writing
feats are the results of conjuring. The process generally
used is the following.

The medium takes two slates, binds them together,
after first having deposited a small bit of chalk or slate
pencil between their surfaces, and either holds them in
his hands, or lays them on the table. Soon the scratching of the pencil is heard, and when the cords are removed a spirit message is found upon the surface of one
of the slates. I will endeavor to explain the "modus
operandi" of these startling experiments.

Some years ago, the most famous of the slate-writing
mediums was Dr. Henry Slade, of New York, with
whom I had several sittings. I was unable to penetrate
the mystery of his performance, until the summer of

1889, when light was thrown upon the subject by the conjurer C— whom I met in Baltimore.

"Do you know the medium Slade?" I asked him.

"Yes," said he, "and he is a conjurer like myself. I've had sittings with him. Come to my rooms to-night, and I will explain the secret workings of the medium's slate-writing. But first I will treat you to a regular séance."

On my way to C's home I tried to put myself in the frame of mind of a genuine seeker after transcendental knowledge. I recalled all the stories of mysterious rappings and ghostly visitations I had read or heard of. It was just the night for such eerie musings. Black clouds were scurrying across the face of the moon like so many mediaeval witches mounted on the proverbial broomsticks *en route* for a mad sabbat in some lonely churchyard. The prestidigitateur's *pension* was a great, lumbering, gloomy old house, in an old quarter of Baltimore. The windows were tightly closed and only the feeble glimmer of gaslight was emitted through the cracks of the shutters. I rang the bell and Mr. C's stage-assistant, a pale-faced young man, came to the door, relieved me of my light overcoat and hat, and ushered me upstairs into the conjurer's sitting-room.

A large, baize-covered table stood in the centre of the apartment, and a cabinet with a black curtain drawn across it occupied a position in a deep alcove. Suspended from the roof of the cabinet was a large guitar. I took a chair and waited patiently for the appearance of the anti-Spiritualist, after having first examined everything in the room—table, cabinet, and musical instruments—but I discovered no evidence of trickery any-where. I waited and waited, but no C—. "Can he have forgotten me?" I said to myself. Suddenly a loud rap resounded on the table top, followed by a succession of raps from the cabinet; and the guitar began to play. I was quite startled. When the music ceased the door opened, and C— entered.

"The spirits are in force to-night," he remarked with a meaning smile, as he slightly diminished the light in the apartment.

"Yes," I replied. "How did you do it?"

"All in good time, my dear ghost-seer," was the an-swer. "Let us try first a few of Dr. Slade's best slate tests."

So saying he handed me a slate and directed me to wash it carefully on both sides with a damp cloth. I did so and passed it back to him. Scattering some tiny fragments of pencil upon it, he held the slate pressed against the under surface of the table leaf, the fingers of his right hand holding the slate, his thumb grasping the leaf. C— then requested me to hold the other end of the slate in a similar fashion, and took my right hand in his left. Heavy raps were heard on the table-top, and I felt the fingers of a spirit hand plucking at my garments from beneath the table. C—'s body seemed possessed with some strange convulsion, his hands quivered, and his eyes had a glassy look. Listening attentively, I heard the sound of a pencil writing on the slate.

"Take care!" gasped the conjurer, breathlessly.

The slate was jerked violently out of our hands by some powerful agency, but the medium regained it, and again pressed it against the table as before. In a little while he brought the slate up and there upon its upper surface was a spirit message, addressed to me—"Are you convinced now?—D. D. Home."

At this juncture there came a knock at the door, and C—, with the slate in his hand, went to see who it was. It proved to be the pale-faced assistant. A few words in a low tone of voice were exchanged between them, and the conjurer returned to the table, excusing the interruption by remarking, "Some one to see me, that is all, but don't hurry, for I have another test to show you." After thoroughly washing both sides of the slate he placed it, with a slate pencil, under a chafing-dish cover in the center of the table. We joined hands and awaited developments.

Being tolerably well acquainted with conjuring devices, I manifested but little surprise in the first test

FIG. 3. THE HOLDING OF THE SLATE.

when the spirit message was written, because the magician *had his fingers on the slate.* But in this test the slate was not in his possession; how then could the writing be accomplished?

"Hush!" said C——, "is there a spirit present?" A responsive rap resounded on the table, and after a few minutes' silence, the mysterious scratching of the slate-pencil began. I was nonplussed.

"Turn over the slate," said the juggler.

I complied with his request and found a long message to me, covering the entire side of the slate. It was signed "Cagliostro."

"What do you think of Dr. Slade's slate tests?" inquired C——.

"Splendid!" I replied, "but how are they done?"

His explanations made the seeming marvel perfectly plain. While the slate is being examined in the first test, the medium slips on a thimble with a piece of slate pencil attached or else has a tiny bit of pencil under his finger nail. In the act of holding the slate under the table, he writes the short message backwards on its under side. It becomes necessary, however, to turn the slate over before exhibiting it to the sitter, so that the writing may appear to have been written on its upper surface—

the side that has been pressed to the table. To accomplish this the medium pretends to go into a sort of neurotic convulsion, during which state the slate is jerked away from the sitter, presumably by spirit power, and is turned over in the required position. It is not immediately brought up for examination but is held for a few seconds underneath the table top, and then produced with a certain amount of deliberation.

The special difficulty of this trick consists in the medium's ability to write in reverse upon the under surface of the slate. If he wrote from left to right, in the ordinary method, it would, of course, reverse the message when the slate is examined, and give a decided clue to the mystery. This inscribing in reverse, or mirror writing, as it is often called, is exceedingly difficult to do, but nothing is impossible to a Slade.

But how is the writing done on the slate in the second test? asks the curious reader. Nothing easier! The servant who raps at the door brings with him, concealed under his coat, a second slate, upon which the long message is written. Over the writing is a pad cut from a book-slate, exactly fitting the frame of the prepared slate. It is impossible to detect the fraud when the light in the room is a trifle obscure. The medium makes an

exchange of slates, returns to the table, washes both sides
of the trick slate, and carelessly exhibits it to the sitter,
the writing being protected of course by the pad. Before placing the slate under the chafing-dish cover, he
lets the pad drop into his lap. Now comes a crucial point
in the imposture : the writing heard beneath the slate,
supposed to be the work of a disembodied spirit. The
medium under cover of his handkerchief removes from
his pocket an instrument known as a "pencil-clamp."
This clamp consists of a small block of wood with two
sharp steel points protruding from the upper edge and a
piece of slate pencil fixed in the lower. The medium
presses the steel points into the under surface of the
table with sufficient force to attach the block securely
to the table, and then rubs a pencil, previously attached
to his right knee by silk sutures, against the side of the
pencil fastened to the apparatus. The noise produced
thereby exactly simulates that of writing upon a slate.
In my case the illusion was perfect. During the examination of the message, the medium has ample opportunity to secrete the false pad and the clamp in his
pocket. Instead of having a servant bring the slate to
him and making the exchange described above, he may
have the trick slate concealed about him before the sé-

ance begins, with the message written on it, and adroitly make the substitution while the sitter is engaged in lowering the light. Dr. Slade almost invariably adopted the first-mentioned exchange, because it enabled his confederate to write a lucid message to the sitter.

An examination of the sitter's overcoat in the hall frequently yielded valuable information in the way of names and initials extracted from letters, sealed or unsealed. Sealed letters? Yes; it is an easy matter to steam a gummed envelope, open it, and seal it again. Another method is to wet the sealed envelope with a sponge dipped in alcohol. The writing will show up tolerably well if written upon a card. In a very short time the envelope will dry and exhibit no evidence of having been tampered with.

And now as to the rest of the phenomena witnessed that evening in C—'s room. The raps on the table top were the result of an ingenious, hidden mechanism, worked by electricity; the mysterious hand that operated under the table was the juggler's right foot. He wore slippers and had the toe part of one stocking cut away. By dropping the slipper from his foot he was enabled to pull the edge of my coat, lift and shove a chair away, and perform sundry other ghostly evolutions, thanks to a well trained big toe. Dr. Slade who was long and lithe of limb, worked this dodge to perfection, prior to the paralytic attack which partly disabled his lower limbs.

The stringed instrument which played in the cabinet was arranged as follows: Inside of the guitar was a small musical box, so arranged that the steel vibrating tongues of the box came in contact with a small piece of writing paper. When the box was set to going by means of an electric current, it closely imitated the twanging of a guitar, just as a sheet of music when laid on the strings of a piano simulates a banjo. This spirit guitar is a very useful instrument in the hands of a medium. It may be made to play when it is attached to a telescopic rod, and waved in phosphorescent curves over the heads of a circle of believers in the dark séance.

I shall now sum up the subject of Dr. Slade's spirit-slate writing, (Fig. 3) and endeavor to show how grossly exaggerated the reports of the medium's performances have been, and the reasons for such misstatements. No one who is not a professional or amateur prestidigitateur can correctly report what he sees at a spiritualistic séance.

It is not so much the swiftness of the hand that counts in conjuring but the ability to force the attention of the spectators in different directions away from the crucial point of the trick. The really important part of the test, then, is hidden from the audience, who imagine they have seen all when they have not. Says Dr. Max Dessoir: "It must therefore be regarded as a piece of rare naiveté if a reporter asserts that in the description of his subjective conclusions he is giving the exact objective processes."

This will be seen in Mr. Davey's experiments. Mr. Davey, a member of the London Society for Psychical Research, and an amateur magician who possessed great dexterity in the slate-writing business, gave a series of exhibitions before a number of persons, but did not inform them that the results were due to prestidigitation. No entrance fee was charged for the séances, but the sitters, who were fully impressed with the genuineness of the affair, were requested to submit written reports of what they had seen. These letters, published in vol. iv of the Proceedings of the Society, are admirable examples of mal-observation, for no one detected Mr. Davey exchanging slates and doing the writing.

"The sources of error," says Dr. Max Dessoir, in an article reproduced in the "Open Court," "through which such strange reports arise, may be arranged in four groups. First, the observer interpolates a fact which did not happen, but which he is led to believe has happened; thus, he imagines he has examined the slate when as a fact he never has. Second, he confuses two similar ideas; he thinks he has carefully examined the slate, when in reality he has only done so hastily, or in ignorance of the point at issue. Third, the witness changes the order of events a little in consequence of a very natural deception of memory; he believes he tested the slate later than he actually did. Fourth and last, he passes over certain details which were purposely described to him as insignificant; he does not notice that the 'medium' asks him to close a window, and that the trick is thus rendered possible."

Similar experiments in slate-writing were conducted by the Seybert Commission with Mr. Harry Kellar, the conjurer, after sittings were had with Dr. Slade, and the magician outdid the medium. The Seybert Commission found none of Slade's tests genuine, and officially denied "the extraordinary stories of his performances with locked slates which constitute a large part of his fame."

Dr. Slade began his Spiritualistic operations in London in the year 1876, and charged a fee of a guinea a head for séances lasting a few minutes. Crowds went to see him and he reaped a golden harvest from the credulous, until the grand fiasco came. Slade was caught in one of his juggling séances and exposed by Prof. Lancaster and Dr. Donkin. The result was a criminal prosecution and a sensational trial lasting three days at the Bow Street Police Court. Mr. Maskelyne, the conjurer, was summoned as an expert witness and performed a number of the medium's tricks in the witness box. The court sentenced Slade to three months' hard labor, but he took an appeal from the magistrate's decision. The appeal was sustained on the ground of a technical flaw in the indictment, and the medium fled to the Continent before new summons could be served. He visited Paris, Leipsic, Berlin, St. Petersburg and other cities, giving séances before Royalty and before distinguished members of scientific societies; and afterwards went to Australia. He made money fast and spent it fast, but it took all of his ingenuity to elude the clutches of the police. In 1892, we find him the inmate of a workhouse in one of our Western towns, penniless, friendless and a lunatic.

Slade's séances with Prof. Zoellner, of Berlin, in 1878, attracted wide attention, and did more to advertise his fame as a medium than anything else in his career.

Zoellner's belief in the genuineness of Slade's mediumistic marvels led him to write a curious work, entitled, "Transcendental Physics," being an inquiry into the "fourth dimension of space." Poor old Zoellner, he was half insane when these séances were held! We have the undisputed authority of the Seybert Commission for the correctness of this statement.

In Hamburg, Dr. Borchert wrote to Slade offering him one thousand marks if he would produce writing between locked slates, similar to the writing alleged to have been executed at the Zoellner séances, but the medium took no notice of the professor's letter. The conjurer, Carl Wilmann, with two friends, had a sitting with Slade, but without satisfactory results for the medium. "Slade," says Wilmann, "was unable to distract my attention from the crucial point of the trick, and threw down the slates on the table in disgust, remarking: 'I can not obtain any results to-day, the power that controls me is exhausted. Come tomorrow!'" That tomorrow never arrived for Willmann and his friends; Slade did not keep his appointment, nor could Wilmann succeed in obtaining another sitting with him. The medium had been warned by friends that Wilmann was an expert professor of legerdemain.

It was in 1886 that Slade created such a furore in Hamburg in Spiritualistic circles. A talented conjurer of that city, named Schradieck, after a few weeks' practice succeeded in eclipsing Slade. He learned to write in reverse on slates, and produced writing in various colored chalks. Another one of his experiments was making the slate disappear from one side of the table where it was held *a la* Slade and appear at the opposite end of the table suddenly, as if held up to view by a spirit hand. Wilmann describes the effect as startling in the extreme and says Schradieck produced it by means of his left foot. After Slade's departure from Hamburg, spirit mediums sprang up like toadstools in a single night. Wilmann in his crusade against these worthies had many interesting experiences. He gives in his work "Moderne Wunder" several exposes of mediumistic tricks, two of which, in the sealed slate line, are very ingenious. The medium takes a slate (one furnished by the sitter if preferred), wipes it on both sides with a wet sponge, and then wraps it up carefully in a piece of ordinary white wrapping paper, allowing the package to be sealed and corded *ad libitum*. Notwithstanding all the precautions used, a message appears on the slate. It is accomplished in this way. A message in reverse is written

on the wrapping paper with a camel's hair brush or
pointed stick, dipped in some sticky substance, and finely
powdered slate pencil dust is scattered over the writing.
At a little distance, especially in a dim light, it is impossible to discover the writing as it blends very well
with the white paper. In wrapping up the slate the medium presses the writing on the paper against the surface of the slate and the chirography adheres thereto,
very much as the greasy drawing on a lithographer's
stone prints on paper.

In the other experiment the medium uses a *papier
mache* slate, set in the usual wooden frame. A *papier
mache* pad is prepared with a spirit message on one surface; on the other is pasted a piece of newspaper. This
pad is laid, written side down, on a sheet of newspaper.
After the genuine slate has been washed, the medium
proceeds to wrap it up in the newspaper, and presses the
trick pad, writing up, into the frame of the slate where
it exactly fits into a groove prepared for the purpose.

Since Dr. Slade's retirement from the mediumistic
field, Pierre L. O. A. Keeler's fame as a slate-writing
medium has been spread broadcast. He oscillates between Boston, New York, Cleveland, Philadelphia, Baltimore and Washington, and has a very large and fash-

ionable *clientele*. He gives evening materializing séances of the cabinet type three times a week at his rooms. During the day he gives private slate tests which are very popular.

I had a sitting with him on the afternoon of April 24th, 1895. In order to gain his confidence, I went as one witnessing a slate séance for the first time, that is, I accepted *his* slates, and had no prepared questions.

I was ushered into a small, back parlor by the medium who closed the folding doors. We were alone. I made a mental photograph of the surroundings. There was no furniture except a table and two chairs placed near the window. Over the table was a faded cloth, hanging some eight or ten inches below the table. Upon it were several pads of paper and a heterogeneous assortment of lead pencils. Leaning against the mantelpiece, within a foot or so of the medium's chair, were some thirty or forty slates.

"Take a seat", said Mr. Keeler pointing to a chair. I sat down, whereupon he seated himself opposite me, remarking as he did so, "Have you brought slates with you?"

"I have not," was my reply.

"Then, if you have no objection," he said, "we will use

two of mine. Please examine these two slates, wash them clean with this damp cloth, and dry them." With that he passed me two ordinary school-slates, which I inspected closely, and carefully cleaned.

"Be kind enough to place the slates to one side," said Keeler. I complied.

"Have you prepared any slips with the names of friends, relatives, or others, who have passed into spirit life, with questions for them to answer?"

"I have not," I replied.

"Kindly do so then," he answered, "and take your time about it. There is a pad on the table. Please write but a single question on each slip. Then fold the slips and place them on the table." I did so.

"I will also make one," he continued, "it is to my spirit control, George Christy." He wrote a name on a slip of paper, folded it, and tossed it among those I had prepared, passing his hand over them and fingering them, saying, "It is necessary to get a psychic impression from them." We sat in silence several minutes.

After a little while Mr. Keeler said: "I do not know whether or not we shall get any responses this afternoon, but have patience." Again we waited. "Suppose you write a few more slips," he remarked, "perhaps we'll

FIG. 4 — SLATE WRITING

have better luck. Be sure and address them to people who were old enough to write before they passed into spirit life." This surprised me, but I complied with his wishes. While writing I glanced furtively at him from time to time; his hands were in his lap, concealed by the table cloth. He looked at me occasionally, then at his lap, fixedly. *I am satisfied that he opened some of my slips, having adroitly abstracted them from the table in the act of fingering them.*

He directed me to take my handkerchief and tie the two slates on the table tightly together, holding the slates in his hands as I did so. I laid the slates on the table before me, and we waited. "I think we will succeed this time in getting responses to some of the questions. Let us hold the slates." He grasped them with fingers and thumbs at one end, and I at the other in like manner, holding the slates about two inches above the table. We listened attentively, and soon was heard the scratching noise of a slate pencil moving upon a slate. The sound seemed directly under the slate, and was sufficiently impressive to startle any person making a slate test for the first time, and unacquainted with the multifarious devices of the sleight-of-hand artist.

"Hold the slates tightly, please!" said Mr. Keeler, as

a convulsive tremor shook his hands. I grasped firmly my end of the slates, and waited further developments. The faint tap of a slate pencil upon a slate was heard, and the medium announced that the communications were finished. I untied the handkerchief, and turned up the inner surfaces of the slates. Upon one of them several messages were written, and signed. Other communications were received during the sitting. After the first messages were received, and while I was engaged in reading them, Keeler quickly picked up a slate from the floor, clapped it upon the clean slate remaining on the table, and requested me to tie the two rapidly together with my handkerchief before the influence was lost. At a signal from him I unfastened the slates and found another set of answers. The same proceeding was gone through for the third set. The imitation of a pencil writing upon a slate was either made by the apparatus, described in the séance with C— in the first part of this chapter, or by some other contrivance; more than likely by simply scratching with his finger on the under surface of the slate. While my attention was absorbed in the act of writing my second set of questions, he prepared answers to two of my first set and substituted a prepared slate for the cleaned slate on the table. *I was sure he was writing under the table; I heard the faint rubbing of a soft bit of pencil upon the surface of a slate. His hands were in his lap and his eyes were fixed downwards.* Several times I saw him put his fingers into his vest pockets, and he appeared to bring up small particles of something, which I believe were bits of the white and colored crayons used in writing the messages. His quiet audacity was surprising. I give below the questions and answers with my comments thereon:

First Slate. Fig. 4.

QUESTION.

To Mamie:—

Tell me the name of your dead brother?

(Signed) Harry R. Evans.

ANSWER.

You must not think of me as one gone forever from you. You have made conditions by and through which I can return to you, and so long as I can do this I can not feel unhappy. So dear one, rest in the assurance that you are helping me, and that I am doing all I can to help you. Let us make the best of it all and help each other as best we can, then all will be well. My home in spirit life is beautiful and awaiting you. I will be the first to greet you. *I have no dead brother. All of us are living.* I am Mamie —. (The medium here cleverly evades giving a name by an equivoque.)

QUESTION.

To Len—

Tell me the cause of your death, and the circumstances surrounding it?

(Signed) Harry R. Evans.

ANSWER.

Harry! I am very glad to see you. I am happy. You must be reconciled, and not mourn me as dead! I will try to come again soon, when I am stronger and tell of my decease. —Len. (He again evades an answer.)

Second Slate. Fig. 5.

QUESTION.

To A. D. B—

When and where did you die?

(Signed) Harry R. Evans.

ANSWER.

This all seems so strange coming back and writing just as one would if they were in the earth life and communicating with a friend. What a blessed privilege it is. I am so happy. Oh, I would not come back. It is so

FIG. 5 — SLATE WRITING.

restful here. No pain or sorrow. Dear, do not think I have forgotten you, I constantly think of you and wish that you, too, might view these lovely scenes of glorious beauty. You must rest with the thought that when your life is ended upon the earth, *I will be the first to meet you.* Now be patient and hopeful until we meet where there is no more parting. I am sincerely, A. D. B. (No answer at all. Observe error in first sentence: "as *one* would if *they* were—." A. D. B. was an educated gentleman, and not given to such ungrammatical expressions.

Third Slate. Fig. 6.

QUESTION.

To B. G.—

Can you recall any of the conversations we had together on the B. and P. R. R. cars?

(Signed) H. R. Evans.

ANSWER.

O my dear one, I can only write a few lines that you may know that I see and hear you as you call upon me. I do not forget you. When I am stronger will come again. I do not know what conversation you refer to in the cars. B. G.

(Again evades answering. B. G. was very much interested in the drama, and talked continuously about the stage.)

QUESTION.

To C. J.—

Where did you die, and from what disease?

(Signed) H. R. Evans.

ANSWER.

I know the days and weeks seem long and lonely to you without me. I do not forget you; am doing the best I can to help you. C. J.—.

(Still another evasion of a straightforward question. The lady in spirit life to whom the question was addressed died of consumption in a Roman Catholic Convent. She was only a society acquaintance of the writer, and not on such terms of intimacy as to warrant Mr. Keeler's reply.)

In one corner of Slate No. 2 was the following, written with a yellow crayon: "This is remarkable. How did you know we could come?—H. K. Evans." Scrawled across the face of Slate No. 3, in red pencil, was a communication from George Christy, Mr. Keeler's spirit control, reading as follows: "Many are here who ——G. C. (George Christy)" (The remainder is so badly written, as to be indecipherable.)

On carefully analyzing the various communications it will be observed that the handwriting of the messages from Mamie— and B G.— are similar, possessing the same characteristics as regards letter formation, etc. It does not require a professional expert in chirography to detect this fact. One and the same person wrote the messages purporting to come from Mamie R—, Len—, B. G.—, C. J.—, and A. D. B. *In fact, the writing on all the slates is, in my opinion, the work of Mr. Pierre Keeler.*

The longer communications were doubtless prepared beforehand, being general in nature and conveying about the same information that any departed spirit might give to any inquiring mortal, but, as will be observed, *giving no adequate answers to the queries,* with the exception of the last two sentences, *which were written by the medium, after he became acquainted with the tenor of the questions upon the folded slips.* The very short communications are written in a careless hand, such as a man would dash off hastily. There is an attempt at disguise, but a clumsy one, the letters still retaining the characteristics of the more deliberate chirography of the long communications. A close inspection of the slates reveals the exact similarity of the y's, u's, I's, g's, h's, m's and n's.

The handwriting of messages on slates should be, and is claimed to be, adequate evidence of the genuineness of the communication, for are we not supposed to know the handwriting of our friends?

Possibly Mr. Keeler would claim that the handwriting was the work of his control "Geo. Christy", who acted as a sort of amanuensis for the spirits. If this be so, why the attempts at *disguise*, and bungling attempts at that?

In the séance with Mr. Keeler, I subjected him to no tests. He had everything his own way. *I should have brought my own marked slates with me and never let them out of my sight for an instant. I should have subjected the table to a close examination, and requested the medium to move or rather myself removed the collection of slates against the mantel, placed so con- veniently within his reach.* I did not do this, because of his well known irascibility. He would probably have shown me the door and refused a sitting on any terms, as he has done to many skeptics. I was anxious to meet Keeler, and preferred playing the novice rather than not get a slate test from one of the best-known and most famous of modern slate-writing mediums.

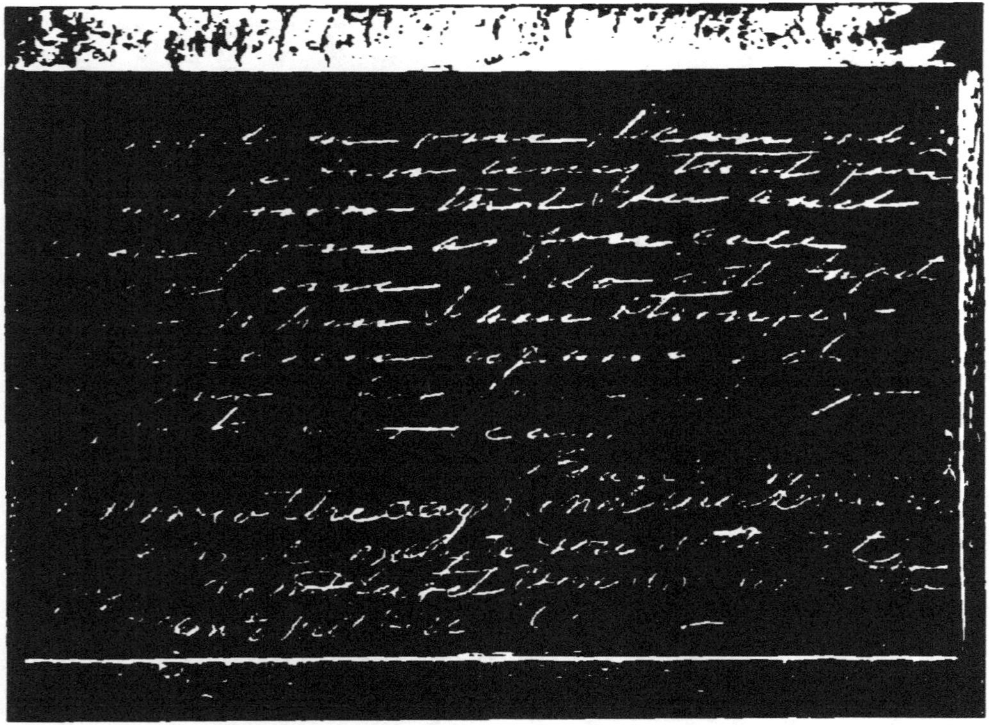

FIG. 6 — SLATE WRITING.

After what has been stated, I think there can be no
shadow of doubt that the medium abstracted by sleight-
of-hand some of the paper slips containing my written
questions, read them under cover of the table, and did the
slate-writing himself. All of these slate-tests, where
pellets or slips of paper are used, are performed in a similar manner, as will be seen from the exposé published
by the Society for Psychical Research. In vol. viii of
the proceedings of that association will be found a
number of revelations, one of which throws considerable light on the Keeler tests. The sitter was Dr.
Richard Hodgson, and the medium was a Mrs. Gillett.
Says Dr. Hodgson:

"Under pretence of 'magnetising' the pellets prepared
by the sitter, or folding them more tightly, she substi-
tutes a pellet of her own for one of the sitter's. Reading
the sitter's pellet below the table, she writes the answer
on one of her own slates, a pile of which, out of the
sitter's view, she keeps on a chair by her side. She
then takes a second slate, places it on the table, and
sponges and dries both sides, after which she takes the
first slate, and turning the side upon which she has
written towards herself, rubs it in several places with a
dry cloth or the ends of her fingers as though cleaning

it. She then places it, writing downward, on the other slate on the table, and sponges and dries the upper surface of it. She then pretends to take one of the pellets on the table and put it between the two slates. What she does, however, is to bring the pellet up from below the table, take another of the sitter's pellets on the table into her hand, and place the pellet which she has brought up from below the table between the slates, keeping in her hand the pellet just taken from the top of the table. The final step is to place a rubber band round both slates, in doing which she turns both slates over together. She professes to get the writing without the use of any chalk or pencil. Some of her slates are prepared beforehand with messages or drawings. More interesting, perhaps, because of its boldness, is her method of producing writing on the sitter's own slates. Under the pretence of 'magnetising' these she cleans them several times, rubs them with her hands, stands them up on end together, and while they are in this position between herself and the sitter she writes with one hand on the slate-side nearest to herself, holding the slates erect with the other hand. Later on, she lays both slates together flat on the table again, the writing being on the undermost surface. She then sponges the upper surface of the top slate, turns it over, and sponges its other surface. She next withdraws the bottom slate, places it on top and sponges its top surface, keeping its under surface carefully concealed. The final step, the reversal, is made, as in the other case, with the help of the rubber band. Mrs. Gillett has probably other methods, also. Those which I have described were all that I witnessed at my single sitting with her."

My friend, Dr. L. M. Taylor, of Washington, D.C., an investigator of Spiritualistic phenomena, and skeptical like myself of the objective phases of the subject, has had many sittings with Keeler for independent slate-writing. One séance in particular he is fond of relating:

"On one occasion, after I had written my slips, folded them up, and tossed them on the table, I said to Keeler who was obtaining his 'psychic' impression of them, 'I wish, if possible, to have a spirit tell me the numbers and the maker's name engraved in my watch. I have never taken the trouble to look at the numbers, consequently I do not know them.' 'Your request is an unusual one,' replied the medium, 'but I will endeavor to gratify it.' We had some conversations on the subject that lasted several minutes. Suddenly he picked up a slate pencil, and scrawled the name, *J. S. Granger* on the upper surface of one of my slates; the two slates had been previously tied together with my handkerchief and laid on the table in front of me. 'You recognize that name, do you not?' asked Keeler. 'Yes,' I replied, 'that is one of the names I wrote on the slips. J. S. Granger was an old friend of mine who died some years ago. He was a brother-in-law of Stephen A. Douglass.' 'If you wish to facilitate matters,' said Keeler, 'place your watch on top of the slates, concealed beneath the handkerchief, otherwise we may have to wait an hour or more without obtaining results, and there are a number of persons waiting for me in the ante-room. My time you see is limited.'

"I detached my watch from its chain, and placed it in the required position. Keeler then took a piece of black cloth, used to clean slates, and laid it over my slates. Finally he requested me to take the covered slates and hold them in my lap. I took care to feel through the cloth that the watch was still beneath the handkerchief. In a short time I was directed to uncover the slates, and untie them, which I did. Upon the inner surface of one of the slates the following message was written: 'Dear Friend, Stephen is with me. I have been through that beautiful watch of yours, and, if I see correctly, the number is 163131. On the inside I see this—E. Howard & Co., Boston, 211327. And then your name as follows: Dr. L. M. Taylor, 1221 Mass. Ave., N. W., Washington, D. C. Signed J. M. Granger.'

"I then compared the name and numbers in my watch with those on the slate, and found the latter correct, with the exception of one number. A relative of mine was present in the room during this séance, and I showed her the communication on the slate. Afterwards we passed the slate to Keeler who examined it closely. When he handed it back to me, I was surprised to see that the incorrect number was mysteriously changed to the proper one."

This is a very interesting test, indeed, because of its apparently impromptu character. I have seen similar feats performed by professional conjurers as well as mediums. A dummy watch is substituted for the sitter's watch, and after the medium has ascertained the name and numbers on the sitter's timepiece, he succeeds in adroitly exchanging it again for the dummy, thanks to the black cloth. The writing on the slate in the above séance was evidently produced in the same way as that described in my sitting with Keeler, after he had ascertained the name on the slip. The name of Stephen, of course, was directly obtained from Dr. Taylor. Not having been an eye witness of Keeler's movements in the watch test, I am unable to say how closely Dr. Taylor's description coincides with the medium's actual operations.

In May, 1897, Mr. Pierre Keeler was in Washington, D.C., as usual. My friend, Dr. Taylor, who was desirous of putting the medium to another crucial test, wrote down a list of names on a sheet of paper—cognomens of ancient Egyptian, Chaldean, and Grecian priests and philosophers—folded the paper, and carefully sealed it in an envelope. He took ten slates with him, all of them marked with a private mark of his own. Mr. Keeler eyed the envelope dubiously, but passed no criticisms on the doctor's precautions to prevent trickery. The two men sat down at a table and waited for the spirits to manifest. Dr. Taylor, on this occasion, was absolutely certain that his slates had not been tampered with, and that the medium had not succeeded in opening the envelope. In a little while the comedy of the pencil-scratching between the tied slates began.

"Ah", exclaimed the physician, "a message at last!" Then he thought to himself, "can the medium possibly have deluded my senses by some hypnotic power, and adroitly opened that envelope without my being aware of the fact? But no, that is impossible!"

Mr. Keeler took the slates away from Dr. Taylor, and quickly opened them, *accidentally* dropping one of them behind the table. In a second, however, he brought up the slate, and remarked: "How awkward of me. I beg your pardon," etc. On the surface of this slate was written the following sentence: "See some other medium; d—n it!—George Christy." Dr. Taylor is positive, as he has repeatedly told me, that this message was not inscribed on his own marked slate, but was written by the medium on one of his own. The exchange, of course, must have been effected in the pretended accidental dropping of the doctor's slate by the medium. This is a very old expedient among pretenders to spirit power. All conjurers are familiar with the device. Imro Fox, the American magician, uses it constantly in his entertainments, with capital effect.

Dr. Taylor, unfortunately, did not succeed in getting possession of the medium's prepared slate. Another exchange was undoubtedly made by Mr. Keeler, and the physician had returned to him his own marked slate. When he got home that afternoon, and had time to carefully scrutinize his slates, he found that they bore no evidence of having been written upon at all. Having also examined these slates, I am prepared to add my testimony to that of Dr. Taylor.

The reader will see from the above-described séance that unless the medium (or a confederate) is enabled to read the names and questions, prepared by the sitter, his hands are practically tied in all experiments in psychography.

When investigators bring their own marked slates with them, screwed tightly together, and sealed, the medium has to adopt different tactics from those employed in the tests before mentioned. He has to call in the aid of a confederate. The audacity of the sealed-slate test is without parallel in the annals of pretended mediumship. For an insight into the secrets of this phase of psychography, the reading public is indebted to a medium, the anonymous author of a remarkably interesting work, "Revelations of a Spirit Medium." Many skeptical investigators have been converted to Spiritualism by these tests. They invariably say to you when approached on the subject: "I took my own marked slates, carefully screwed together, to the medium, and had lengthy messages written upon them by spirit power. *These slates never left my hands for a second.*" I will quote what the writer of "Revelations of a Spirit Medium" says on the subject:

"No man ever received independent slate-writing between slates fastened together that he did not allow out of his hands a few seconds. Scores of persons will tell you that they *have* received writing under those conditions through the mediumship of the writer; but the writer will tell you how he fooled them and how you can do so if you see fit.

"In the first place you will rent a house with a cellar in connection. Cut a trap-door one foot square through the floor between the sills on which the floor is laid. Procure a fur floor mat with long hair. Cut a square out of the mat and tack it to the top of the trap door. Tack the mat fast to the floor, for some one may visit you who will want to raise it up.

"Explain the presence of the fur by saying it is an absorbent of magnetic forces, through which you produce the writing. Over the rug place a heavy pine table about four feet square; and over the table a heavy cover that reaches the floor on all sides. Put your assistant in the cellar with a coal-oil stove, a tea-kettle of hot water, different colored letter wax and lead pencils, a screw driver, a pair of nippers, a pair of pliers, a pair of scissors and an assortment of wire brads. You are ready for business.

"When your sitter comes in you will notice his slates, if he brings a pair, and see if they are secured in any way that your man in the cellar can not duplicate. If they are, you can touch his slates with your finger and say to him that you can not use his slates on account of the 'magnetism' with which they are saturated. He will know nothing of 'magnetic conditions' and will ask you what he is to do about it.

"You will furnish him a pair of new slates with water and cloths to clean them. You also furnish him paper to write his questions on and the screws, wax, paper and mucilage to secure them with. He will write his questions and fasten the slates securely together.

"You now conduct him to your séance-room and invite inspection of your table and surroundings. After the examination has been made you will seat the sitter at one side of the table with his side and arm next it. If he desires to keep hold of the slates a signal agreed upon between yourself and your assistant will cause the spirit in the cellar to open the trap door, which opens downwards, and to push through the floor and into position where the sitter can grasp one end of it, a pair of dummy slates. This dummy your assistant will continue to hold until the sitter has taken hold of it after the following performance:

"Your assistant lets you know everything is ready by touching your foot. You now reach and take the sitter's slates and put them below the table, and under it, telling the sitter to put his hand under from his side and hold them with you. He puts his hand under and gets hold of the dummy slates held by your assistant.

"Your assistant holds on until you have stood the slates on end, leaning against the table leg, and have got hold of the dummy. He then takes the sitter's slates below and closes the trap. He proceeds to open them, read the questions, answer them and refasten the slates.

"You will be entertaining your sitter by twitching and jerking and making clairvoyant and clairaudient guesses for him.

"When your assistant touches your foot you will know that he is ready to make the exchange again, by which the sitter will get hold of the slates he fastened. When you get the signal you give a snort and jump that jerks the end of the slates from the sitter's hand. He is now given the end of the slates held by your assistant, and you will allow the assistant to take the dummy. After sitting a moment or two longer, you will tell the sitter to take out his slates and examine them if he chooses. Many times they do not open the slates until they reach their homes.

"This, reader, is the man who will declare that he furnished the slates and did not allow them out of his hands a minute.

"The usual method of obtaining the writing is for the medium to hold the slates alone. When this is the case the medium passes the slates below, and receives in return a dummy which he is continually thumping on the under side of the table for the purpose of showing the sitter that the slates are there all the time.

"It is not necessary that you should use a cellar to get this phase of 'independent slate-writing.' You could place your table against a partition door and by fitting one of the small panels with hinges and bolts, would have a very convenient way of obtaining the assistance of the spirit in the next room. It is also possible to make a trap in a room that has a wooden wainscoting."

Before closing this brief survey of slate-writing experiments, I must describe an exceedingly ingenious trick, indeed, bordering on the marvelous. It is the recent invention of a Western conjurer, and solves the problem of actually writing between locked slates by physical means. The effect is as follows: You request the sitter to take two slates, wash them carefully, and tie them together, after first having placed a bit of chalk between their surfaces. Hold them under the table for a minute, and then hand them to the sitter for examination. A name, or a short sentence, in answer to some question, will be found scrawled across the upper surface of the bottom slate. It is accomplished in this way. You take a small pellet of iron or steel, coat it with mucilage, and dip it into chalk or slate-pencil dust. This dust will adhere and harden into a consistent mass, after a little while, completely concealing the metal, and causing the whole to resemble a bit of chalk. Take this supposed pellet of chalk from your vest pocket and place it between the slates; hold the latter level beneath a table, and by moving the poles of a strong magnet against the surface of the under slate, you can cause the iron or steel to write a name or sentence, thanks to its coating of chalk dust. It is better to use slates with rather deep frames, in order that the chalked metal may write with facility. It requires considerable practice to write with ease in the manner described above. The first thing of course is to locate the position of the chalk between the locked slates. · To enable you to do this, place the supposed chalk in one corner of slate No. 1 before covering with slate No. 2, or else exactly in the center of slate No. 2. In this way you will have no difficulty in affecting the metal with the magnet, when the slates are held under the table. There are various ways of holding the slates; one, is to ask the sitter to hold one end, while you hold the other, five or six inches above the table. The light is put out, and you take the magnet from your pocket and execute the writing. The noise of the magnet passing over the surface of the under slate serves to represent a disembodied spirit as doing the writing.

2. The Master of the Mediums.

One of the most remarkable personalities serving as an exponent of Spiritualism was Daniel Dunglas Home, the Napoleon of necromancy, and the Past Grand Master of Mediums. His career reads like a romance. He lived in a sort of twilight land, and hob-nobbed with kings, queens and other people of noble blood.

"Something unsubstantial, ghostly,

   Seems this Theurgist,

   In deep meditation mostly

   Wrapped, as in a mist.

   Vague, phantasmal and unreal,

   To our thoughts he seems,

   Walking in a world ideal,

   In a land of dreams."

He wound his serpentine way into the best society of London, Paris, Berlin, Rome, and St. Petersburg—"always despising filthy lucre," as Maskelyn remarks, "but never refusing a diamond worth ten times the amount he would have received in cash, or some present, which the host of the house at which he happened to be manifesting always felt constrained to offer."

This thaumaturgist of the Nineteenth Century was born near Edinburg, Scotland, on March 20, 1833, and came of a family reported to be gifted with "second sight." His father, William Home, was a natural son of Alexander, tenth Earl of Home. Strange phenomena occurred during the medium's childhood. At the age of nine he was adopted by his aunt, Mrs. McNeill Cook, who brought him to America. He began giving séances about the year 1852. Among the notable men who attended these early "sittings" were William Cullen Bryant, Professors Wells and Hare, and Judge Edmonds.

Home had a tall, slight figure, a fair and freckled face —before disease made it the color of yellow wax—keen, slaty-blue eyes, thin bloodless lips, a rather snub nose, and curly auburn hair. His manners, though forward, were agreeable, and he recited such poetry as Poe's "Raven" and "Ulalume" with powerful effect. He was altogether a weird sort of personage. His principal mediumistic manifestations were rappings, table-tipping, ghostly materializations, playing on sealed musical instruments, levitation, and handling fire with impunity.

In 1855 he launched his necromantic bark on European waters. No man since Cagliostro ever created so profound a sensation in the Old World. He wrote his reminiscences in two large volumes, but little credence

can be given them, as they are full of extravagant statements and wild fantasies.

The London *Punch* (May 9th, 1868), printed the following effusion on the medium, a sort of parody on
"Home, Sweet Home:"

Through realms Thaumaturgic the student may roam,
And not light on a worker of wonders like *Home*.
Cagliostro himself might descend from his chair,
And set up our *Daniel* as Grand-Cophta there—
　Home, *Home*, *Dan. Home*,
　No medium like *Home*.

Spirit legs, spirit hands, he gives table and chair;
Gravitation defying, he flies in the air;
But the fact to which henceforth his fame should be
　pinned,
Is his power to raise, not himself but the wind!—
　Home, *Home*, *Dan. Home*,
　No medium like *Home*:

Robert Browning made him the subject of his celebrated satirical poem, "Mr. Sludge, the Medium."

Some of the most celebrated scientific and literary
personages of England became interested in his mysterious abilities, and among his intimate friends were the

Earl of Dunraven, Mary Howitt, Mrs. S. C. Hall, Prof. Wallace, and Sir Edward Bulwer-Lytton. There is good authority for believing that Home was the mysterious Margrave of Bulwer's weird novel, "A Strange Story." Bulwer was an ardent believer in the supernatural and Home spent many days at Knebworth amid a select coterie of ghost-seers. The famous novelist relates that as Home sat with him in the library of Knebworth, conversing upon politics, social matters, books or other chance topics, the chairs rocked and the tables were suspended in mid-air.

When the medium was requested to exert his power and found himself in condition, it is alleged, he would rise and float about the room. This in Spiritualistic parlance is termed "levitation". At Knebworth and other places, some of the most prominent people of the day claim to have seen Home lift himself up and sail tranquilly out of a window, around the house, and come in by another window.

The Earl of Dunraven told many stories equally strange of performances that were given in his presence. The Earl declared that he had many times seen Home elongate and shorten his body, and cause the closed piano to play by putting his fingers on the lid.

FIG. 7 — HOME AT THE TUILERIES.

In the autumn of 1855 the famous medium went to Florence; there, also, the spirit manifestations secured him the *entrec* into the best society of the old Italian city. In his memoirs he speaks of an incident occurring through his mediumship, at a séance given in Florence: "Upon one occasion, while the Countess C— was seated at one of Erard's grand-action pianos, it rose and balanced itself in the air, during the whole time she was playing." An English lady, resident at Florence, in a supposed haunted house, procured the services of Home to exorcise the ghost. They sat at a table in the sitting-room, and raps were heard proceeding from that piece of furniture, and rustling sounds in the room as of a person moving about in a heavy garment. The spirit being adjured in the name of the "Holy Trinity" to leave the premises, the demonstrations ceased.

In February, 1856, the medium joined the retinue of Count B—, a Polish nobleman, and went to Naples with his patron. From Naples to Rome was the next step, and, in the Eternal City, the medium joined the Romish Church, and was adjured by the Pope to abandon spirit séances forever. In 1858 we find Home in St. Petersburg, where he married the youngest daughter of General Count de Kroll, of Russia, and a goddaughter of the

Emperor Nicholas, the marriage taking place on Sunday, August 1, 1858, in the private chapel attached to the house of the lady's brother-in-law, the Count Gregoire Koucheleff-Besborodko. It was a very notable affair, and Alexander Dumas came from Paris to attend the ceremony. Home's spirit power which had left him since his conversion to the Roman Catholic faith now returned in full force, it is said, and he saw standing near him at the wedding the spirit form of his mother. In 1862 his wife died at the Chateau Laroche, near Perigneux, France, and the medium repaired to Rome for the purpose of studying sculpture. The reports of the spirit phenomena constantly attending Home's presence reached the ears of the Papal authorities and he was compelled to leave the city, notwithstanding the fact that he gave positive assurance that he would give no séance. He was actually charged with being a sorcerer, like Cagliostro, an accusation that reads very strange in the Nineteenth Century. This affair embittered Home against the Church, and he abandoned Roman Catholicism for the Greek Church.

After the Roman fiasco, the famous medium returned to England to give Spiritualistic lectures and séances. A writer in *"All the Year Round"*, gives the following pen picture of the medium, as he appeared in 1866: "He is a tall, thin man, with broad square shoulders, suggestive of a suit of clothes hung upon an iron cross. His hair is long and yellow; his teeth are large, glittering and sharp; his eyes are a pale grey, with a redness about the eye-lids, which comes and goes in a ghastly manner, as he talks. When he shows his glittering sharp teeth, and that red line comes round his slowly rolling eyes, he is not a pleasant sight to look upon. His hands are long, white and bony, and on taking them you discover that they are icy cold." A *suit of clothes hung upon an iron cross* is a weird touch in this pen picture.

Home about this time intended going upon the stage, but abandoned the idea to become the secretary of the "Spiritual Atheneum", a society formed for the investigation of psychic phenomena.

One of the most notable passages in the life of the great medium was the famous law suit in which he was concerned in England. In 1866 he became acquainted with a wealthy lady, Mrs. Jane Lyons. In his role of medium she consulted him constantly about the welfare of her husband in the spirit world, and her business affairs. She gave him £33,000 for his services. Relatives and friends of Mrs. Lyons, however, saw in Home a cunning adventurer who was preying upon a weak-minded woman. A suit was instituted against the medium to recover the money, and the case became a *cause celebre* in the annals of the English courts.

In the autumn of 1871, Home, who before that time, had been quite a "lion" at the court of Napoleon III and Eugene, followed the German army from Sedan to Versailles, and was hand-in-glove with the King of Prussia. His second marriage took place in October, 1871, at Paris, and after a brief honeymoon in England he visited St. Petersburg with his wife, who was a member of the noble Russian family of Alsakoff.

On the 21st of June, 1886, the great American ghost-seer died of consumption, at Auteuil, near Paris, France. For years he was out of health, and he ascribed his weakness to the expenditure of vital force in working wonders during the earlier part of his career.

He was buried at St. Germain-en-Laye, with the rites of the Russian Church. The funeral was a very simple one, not more than twenty persons being present, all of whom were in full evening dress. The idea was to emphasize the Spiritualists' belief that death is not a subject for mourning, but is liberation, an occasion for rejoicing.

The curious reader will find many accounts of Home's invulnerability to fire while in the trance state, notably those of Prof. Crookes, contained in the proceedings of the Society for Psychical Research. In the March, 1868, number of *"Human Nature,"* Mr. H. D. Jencken writes as follows concerning a séance given by the medium:

"Mr. Home, (after various manifestations) said, 'we have gladly shown you our power over fluids, we will now show you our power over solids.' He then knelt down before the hearth, and deliberately breaking up a glowing piece of coal in the fire place, took up a largish lump of incandescent coal and placing the same in his left hand, proceeded to explain that caloric had been extracted by a process known to them (the spirits), and that the heat could in part be returned. This he proved by alternately cooling and heating the coal; and to convince us of the fact, allowed us to handle the coal which had become cool, then suddenly resumed its heat sufficient to burn one, as I again touched it. I examined Mr. Home's hand, and quite satisfied myself that no artificial means had been employed to protect the skin, which did not even retain the smell of smoke. Mr. Home then reseated himself, and shortly awoke from his trance quite pale and exhausted."

Other witnesses of the above experiment were Lord Lindsay, Lord Adare, Miss Douglas, Mr. S. C. Hall, Mr. W. H. Harrison and Prof. Wallace. Mr. H. Nisbet, of Glasgow, relates (*Human Nature*, Feb. 1870) that in his own home in January, 1870, Mr. Home took a red hot coal from the grate and put it in the hands of a lady and gentleman to whom it felt only warm. Subsequently he placed the same on a folded newspaper, the result being a hole burnt through eight layers of paper. Taking another blazing coal he laid it on the same journal, and carried it around the apartment for upwards of three minutes, without scorching the paper.

Among the crowned heads and famous people before whom Mr. Home appeared were Napoleon III and the Empress Eugénie, Queen Victoria, King Louis I and King Maximilian of Bavaria, the Emperor of Russia, the King and Queen of Wurtemberg, the Duchess of Hamilton, the Crown Prince of Prussia and old Gen. Von Moltke. Alexander Dumas the elder, was a constant companion of the medium for a long time, and wrote columns about him.

Napoleon III had two sittings with Home—and it is

said Home materialized the spirit of the first Napoleon, who appeared in his familiar cocked hat, gray overcoat and dark green uniform with white facings. "My fate?" asked Louis, trembling with awe. "Like mine—discrowned, and death in exile," replied the ghost; then it vanished. The Empress swooned and Napoleon III fell back in his chair as if about to faint. The medium in his first séance with the French Emperor succeeded only in materializing some flowers and a spirit hand, which the Emperor was permitted to grasp.

Celia Logan, the journalist, in writing of one of Home's s ances at a nobleman's house in London, says:

"On this occasion the medium announced that he would produce balls of fire and illuminated hands. Failing in the former, he declared that the spirits were not strong enough for that to-night, and so he would have to confine himself to showing the luminous hands.

"The house was darkened and Home groped his way alone to the head of the broad staircase, where every few minutes a pair of luminous hands were thrown up. The audience was satisfied generally. One lady, however, was not, and whispered to me—she was a half-hearted Spiritualist—that it looked to her as if he had rubbed his own hands over with lucifer matches.

"The host stood near the mantel piece and had seen Home abstractedly place a small bottle upon it when he left the room for the staircase. That bottle the host quietly slipped into his pocket. Upon examination the next day it was found to contain phosphorated olive oil or some similar preparation.

"The host had declared himself to have seen Home float through the air from one side of the room to the other, lift a piano several feet in the air by simply placing a finger upon it, and had seen him materialize disembodied spirits; but after the discovery of the phosphorus trick he dropped Home at once."

It is a significant fact that the medium while giving séances in Paris in 1857 refused to meet Houdin, the renowned prestidigitateur.

I shall now attempt an exposé of Home's physical phenomena. Home's extraordinary feat of alternately cooling and heating a lump of coal taken from a blazing fire, as related by Mr. H. D. Jencken and others, is easily explained. It is a juggling trick. The "coal" is a piece of spongy platinum which bears a close resemblance to a lump of half burnt coal, and is palmed in the hand, as a prestidigitateur conceals a coin, a pack of cards, an egg, or a small lemon. The medium or magician ad-

vances tò the grate and pretends to take a genuine lump
of coal from the fire but brings up instead, at the tips of
his fingers, the piece of platinum., In a secret breast
pocket of his coat he has a small reservoir of hydrogen,
with a tube coming down the sleeve and terminating an
inch or so above the cuff. By means of certain mechanical arrangements, to enable him to let on and off the gas
at the proper moment, he is able to accomplish the trick;
for when a current of hydrogen is allowed to impinge
upon a piece of spongy platinum, the metal becomes incandescent, and as soon as the current is arrested the
platinum is restored to its normal condition.

The hand may be protected from burning in various ways, one method being the repeated appli-
cation of sulphuric acid to the skin, whereby it
is rendered impervious to the action of fire for
a short period of time; another, by wearing
gloves of amianthus or asbestos cloth. With the
latter, worn in a badly lighted room, the medium, without much risk of discovery, can handle red hot coals or
iron with impunity. The gloves may at the proper
moment be slipped off and concealed about the person.
A small slip of amianthus cloth placed on a newspaper
would protect it from a hot coal and the same means

could be used when a coal is placed in another's hand or upon his head.

As to the marvelous "levitation", either the witnesses of the alleged feat were under some hypnotic spell, or else they allowed their imaginations to run riot when describing the event. In the case of Lord Lindsay and Lord Adare, D. Carpenter in his valuable paper "On Fallacies Respecting the Supernatural" (*Contemporary Review*, Jan., 1876) says: "A whole party of believers affirm that they saw Mr. Home float out of one window and in at another, while a single honest skeptic declares that Mr. Home was sitting in his chair all the time." It seems that there were three gentlemen present besides the medium when the alleged phenomenon took place, the two noblemen and a "cousin". It is this unnamed hard-headed cousin to whom Dr. Carpenter refers as the "honest skeptic."

Many of Home's admirers have declared that he possessed the power of mesmerizing certain of his friends. These gentlemen were no doubt hypnotized and related honestly what they believed they had seen. Again, the expectancy of attention and the nervous tension of the average sitter in spirit-circles tend to produce a morbidly impressible condition of mind. Many mediums since

Home's day have performed the act of levitation, but always in a dark room. Mr. Angelo Lewis, the writer on magic, reveals an ingenious method by which levitation is effected. When the lights are extinguished the medium—who, by the way, must be a clever ventriloquist—removes his boots and places them on his hands.

"I am rising, I am rising, but pay no attention", he remarks, as he goes about the apartment, where the sitters are grouped in a circle about him, and he lightly touches the heads of various persons. A shadowy form is dimly seen and a smell of boot leather becomes apparent to the olfactory senses of many present. People jump quickly to conclusions in such matters and argue that where the feet of the medium are, his body must surely be—namely, floating in the air. The illusion is further enhanced by the performers ventriloquial powers. "I am rising! I am touching the ceiling!" he exclaims, imitating the sound of a voice high up. When the lights are turned up, the medium is seen (this time with his boots on his feet) standing on tip-toe, as if just descended from the ceiling.

Sometimes before performing the levitation act, he will say, "In order to convince any skeptic present, that I really float upwards, I will write the initials of my name, or the name of some one present, on the ceiling." When the lights are raised, the letters are seen written on the ceiling in a bold scrawling hand. How is it done? The medium has concealed about him a telescopic steel rod, something like those Chinese fishing rods at one time in vogue among modern disciples of Izaak Walton. This convenient rod when not in use folds up in a very small compass, but when it is shoved out to its full length, some three or four feet, with a bit of black chalk attached, the writing on the ceiling is easily produced. The magicians of ancient Egypt displayed their mystic rods as a part of their paraphernalia, while the modern magi bear theirs in secret. A tambourine, a guitar, a bell, or a spirit hand, rubbed with phosphorus, may also be fixed to this ingenious appliance, and floated over the heads of the spectators, and even a horn may be blown, through the hollow rod.

The materialization of a spirit hand which crept from beneath a table-cover, and showed itself to the "believers," was one of the most startling things in the repertoire of D. D. Home, as it was in that of Dr. Monck's, an English medium. An explanation of Monck's method of producing the hand may, perhaps, throw some light on Home's "materialization." A small dummy hand, artistically executed in wax, with the fingers slightly bent, is fastened to a broad elastic band about three feet in length. This band is attached to a belt about the performer's waist and passes down his left trouser leg, allowing the hand to dangle within the trouser a few inches above the ankle. I must not forget to explain that to the wrist of the hand is appended an elastic sleeve about five inches long. The medium and two sitters take their seats at a square table, with an over-hanging table-cloth: No one is allowed to be seated at the same side of the table with the medium. This is an imperative condition.

"Diminish the light, please," says the medium. Some one rises to lower the gas to the required dim religious light necessary to all spirit séances. "A little lower, please! Lower, lower still!" remarks the medium. Out the light goes. "Dear, me, but this is vexatious! Somebody light it again and be more careful!" he ejaculates. Under cover of the darkness the agile operator crosses his left foot over his right knee, pulls down the wax hand and fixes it to the toe of his boot by means of the elastic sleeve, the apparatus being masked from the sitters by the table cloth until the time comes for the spirit materialization. The three men place their hands on the table and wait patiently for developments. Presently a rap is heard under the table—disjointed knee of the medium,—and then *mirabile dictu!* the table-cloth shakes and a delicate female hand emerges and shows itself above the edge of the table. A guitar being placed close to the fingers, they soon strum the strings, or rather appear to do so, the medium being the *deus ex machina.* The cleverest part of the whole performance is the fact that the medium never takes his hands from the table. He quietly puts his left foot down on the floor and places his right foot heavily on the false hand—off it comes from the left foot and shoots up the trouser leg like lightning. The sitters may look under the table but they see nothing.

An ingenious improvement has been made to this hand-test by an American conjurer, one that enables the medium to produce the hand although his feet are secured by the sitter. "Be kind enough, sir," says the performer to the investigator, "to place your feet on mine. If I should move my feet ever so little, you would know it, would you not?" The sitter replies in the affirmative. The medium, as soon as he feels the pressure of the sitter's feet, withdraws his right foot from a steel

shape made in imitation of the toe of his boot, and oper-
ates the spirit hand at his leisure. After the sitting, he
of course, inserts his right foot into the shape and carries
it off with him.

The production of spirit music was one of Home's
favorite experiments. There are all sorts of ways of
producing this music, the most ingenious of which I
give:

The apparatus consists of a small circular musical
box, wound up by clock woik, and made to play whenever pressure is put upon a stud projecting a quarter
of an inch from its surface. This box is strapped
around the right leg of the medium just above his
knee, and hidden beneath the trouser leg. When not
in use it is on the under side of the leg. On the table
a musical box is placed and covered with a soup
tureen, or the top of a chafing dish. When the spectators are seated, the medium works the concealed
musical box around to the upper part of his leg near
the knee cap, and by pressing the stud against the
under surface of the table, starts the music playing.
In this way the second musical box seems to play and
the acoustic effect is perfect. Perhaps Home used a

similar contrivance; Dr. Monck did, and was caught in the act by the chief of the Detective Police.

Home during his séances on the Continent of Europe was accused of all sorts of trickery. Some asserted that he had concealed about him a small but powerful electric battery for producing certain illusions, mechanical contrivances attached to his legs for making spirit raps, and last but not least, as the medium states in his "Memoirs:" "they even accused me of carrying a small monkey about with me, concealed, trained to perform all sorts of ghostly tricks."

People also accused him of obtaining a great deal of his information about the spirits of the departed from tombstones like an Old Mortality, and bribing family servants. A more probable explanation may be found perhaps in telepathy.

There is one more phase of Home's mediumship, the moving of heavy pieces of furniture without physical contact, that must be spoken of. In mentioning it, Dr. Max Dessoir, author of the "Psychology of Conjuring,"* says: "We must admit that *a few* feats, such as those of Prof. Crookes with Home, concerning the possibility of setting inanimate objects in

*Introduction to Herrmann the Magician, his Life, his Secrets, (Laird & Lee, Publishers.)

motion without touching them, *appear* to lie entirely outside the sphere of jugglery." In the year 1871, Prof. William Crookes, (now Sir William Crookes) Fellow of the Royal Society, a very eminent scientist, subjected Home to some elaborate tests in order to prove or disprove by means of scientific apparatus the reality of phenomena connected with variations in the weight of bodies, with or without contact. He declared the tests to be entirely satisfactory, but ascribed the phenomena not to spiritual agency, but to a new force, "in some unknown manner connected with the human organization," which for convenience he called the "Psychic Force." He said in his "Reseaches in the Phenomena of Spiritualism:" "Of all the persons endowed with a powerful development of this Psychic Force, and who have been termed 'mediums' upon quite another theory of its origin, Mr. Daniel Dunglas Home is the most remarkable, and it is mainly owing to the many opportunities I have had of carrying on my investigations in his presence that I am enabled to affirm so conclusively the existence of this force." Prof. Crookes' experiments were conducted, as he says, in the full light, and in the presence of witnesses, among them being the famous English barrister, Sergeant Cox, and the astronomer, Dr. Huggins. Heavy articles became light and light articles heavy when the medium came near them. In some cases he lightly touched them, in others refrained from contact.

The first piece of the apparatus constructed by

FIG. 8. CROOKES' APPARATUS.

Crookes to test this psychic force consisted of a mahogany board 36 inches long by 9½ inches wide and 1 inch thick. A strip of mahogany was screwed on at one end, to form a foot, the length being equal to the width of the board. This end of the board was placed on a table, while the other end was upheld by a spring balance, fastened to a strong tripod stand, as will be seen in Fig. 8.

"Mr. Home," writes Prof. Crookes, "placed the tips of his fingers lightly on the extreme end of the mahogany board which was resting on the support, whilst Dr. A. B. [Dr. Huggins] and myself sat, one on each side of it, watching for any effect which might be produced. Almost immediately the pointer of the balance was seen to descend. After a few seconds it rose again. This movement was repeated several times, as if by successive waves of the psychic force. The end of the board was observed to oscillate slowly up and down during the experiment.

"Mr. Home now, of his own accord, took a small hand-bell and a little card match-box, which happened to be near, and placed one under each hand, to satisfy us, as he said, that he was not producing the downward pressure. The very slow oscillation of the spring balance became more marked, and Dr. A. B., watching the index, said that he saw it descend to $6\frac{1}{4}$ lbs. The normal weight of the board as so suspended being 3 lbs., the additional downward pull was therefore $3\frac{1}{4}$ lbs. On looking immediately afterwards at the automatic register, we saw that the index had at one time descended as low as 9 lbs., showing a maximum pull of 6 lbs. upon a board whose normal weight was 3 lbs.

"In order to see whether it was possible to produce much effect on the spring balance by pressure at the place where Mr. Home's fingers had been, I stepped upon the table and stood on one foot at the end of the board. Dr. A. B., who was observing the index of the balance, said that the whole weight of my body (140 lbs.) so applied only sunk the index $1\frac{1}{2}$ lbs., or 2 lbs. when I jerked up and down. Mr. Home had been sitting in a low easy-chair, and could not, therefore, had he tried his utmost, have exerted any material influence on these results. I need scarcely add that his feet as well as his hands were closely guarded by all in the room."

The next series of experiments is thus described:

"On trying these experiments for the first time, I thought that actual contact between Mr. Home's hands and the suspended body whose weight was to be altered was essential to the exhibition of the force; but I found afterwards that this was not a necessary condition, and I therefore arranged my apparatus in the following manner:—

"The accompanying cuts (Figs. 9, 10 and 11) explain the arrangement. Fig. 9 is a general view, and Figs. 10 and 11 show the essential parts more in detail. The reference letters are the same in each illustration. A B is a mahogany board, 36 inches long by $9\frac{1}{2}$ inches wide, and 1 inch thick. It is suspended at the end, B, by a spring balance, C, furnished with an automatic

FIG. 9. CROOKES' APPARATUS.

register, D. The balance is suspended from a very firm tripod support, E.

"The following piece of apparatus is not shown in the figures. To the moving index, O, of the spring balance, a fine steel point is soldered, projecting horizontally outwards. In front of the balance, and firmly fastened to it, is a grooved frame, carry-

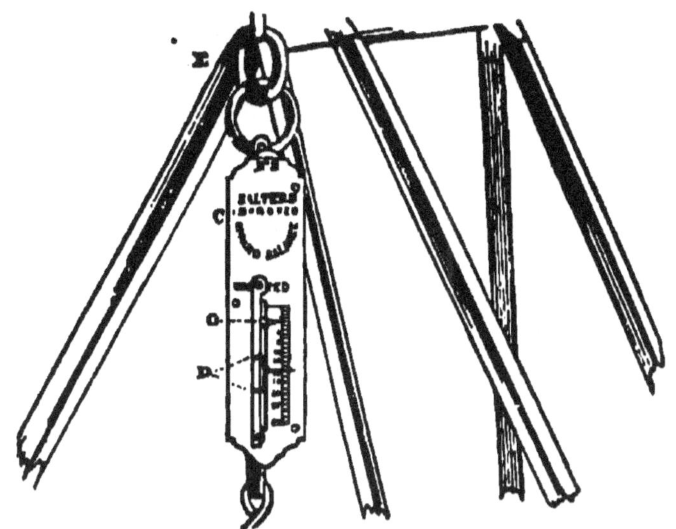

FIG. 10. CROOKES' APPARATUS.

ing a flat box similar to the dark box of a photographic camera. This box is made to travel by
clock-work horizontally in front of the moving index,
and it contains a sheet of plate-glass which has been
smoked over a flame. The projecting steel point im-
presses a mark on this smoked surface. If the balance is at rest, and the clock set going, the result is a
perfectly straight horizontal line. If the clock is
stopped and weights are placed on the end, B, of
the board, the result is a vertical line, whose length
depends on the weight applied. If, whilst the clock
draws the plate along, the weight of the board (or the
tension on the balance) varies, the result is a curved

line, from which the tension in grains at any moment during the continuance of the experiments can be calculated.

"The instrument was capable of registering a diminution of the force of gravitation as well as an increase; registrations of such a diminution were frequently obtained. To avoid complication, however, I will here refer only to results in which an increase of gravitation was experienced.

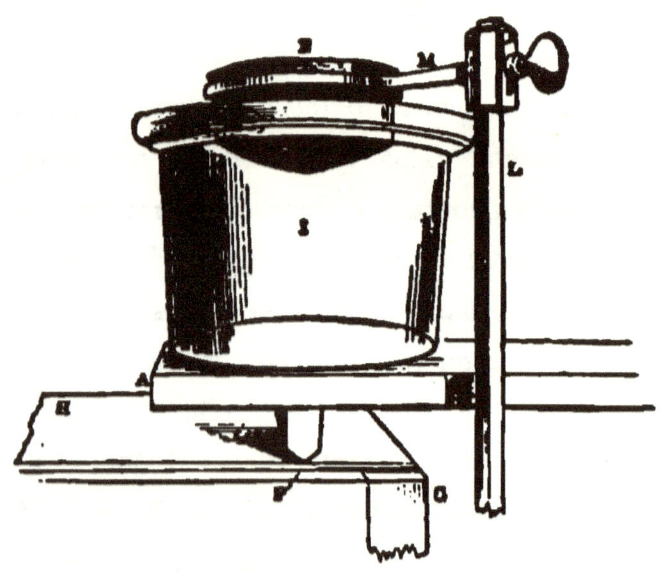

FIG. 11. CROOKES' APPARATUS.

"The end, B, of the board being supported by the spring balance, the end, A, is supported on a wooden strip, F, screwed across its lower side and cut to a knife edge (see Fig. 11). This fulcrum rests on a firm and heavy wooden stand, G H. On the board, exactly over the fulcrum, is placed a large glass vessel filled with water. I L is a massive iron stand, furnished with an arm and a ring, M N, in which rests a hemispherical copper vessel perforated with several holes at the bottom.

"The iron stand is 2 inches from the board, A B, and the arm and copper vessel, M N, are so adjusted that the latter dips into the water $1\frac{1}{2}$ inches, being $5\frac{1}{2}$ inches from the bottom of I, and 2 inches from its circumference. Shaking or striking the arm, M, or the vessel, N, produces no appreciable mechanical effect on the board, A B, capable of affecting the balance. Dipping the hand to the fullest extent into the water in N does not produce the least appreciable action on the balance.

"As the mechanical transmission of power is by this means entirely cut off between the copper vessel and the board, A B, the power of muscular control is thereby completely eliminated.

"For convenience I will divide the experiments into groups, 1, 2, 3, etc., and I have selected one special instance in each to describe in detail. Nothing, however, is mentioned which has not been repeated more than once, and in some cases verified, in Mr. Home's absence, with another person, possessing similar powers.

"There was always ample light in the room where the experiments were conducted (my own dining-room) to see all that took place.

"*Experiment I.*—The apparatus having been properly adjusted before Mr. Home entered the room, he was brought in, and asked to place his fingers in the water in the copper vessel, N. He stood up and dipped the tips of the fingers of his right hand in the water, his other hand and his feet being held. When he said he felt a power, force, or influence, proceeding from his hand, I set the clock going, and almost immediately the end, B, of the board was seen to descend slowly and remain down for about 10 seconds; it then descended a little further, and afterwards rose to its normal height. It then descended again, rose suddenly, gradually sunk for 17 seconds, and finally rose to its normal height, where it remained till the experiment was concluded. The lowest point marked on the glass was equivalent to a direct pull of about

5,000 grains.   The accompanying Figure 12 is a copy
of the curve traced on the glass.

"*Experiment II.*—Contact through water having
proved to be as effectual as actual mechanical contact, I wished to see if the power or force could affect
the weight, either through other portions of the apparatus or through the air.   The glass vessel and iron
stand, etc., were therefore removed, as an unnecessary
complication, and Mr. Home's hands were placed on the

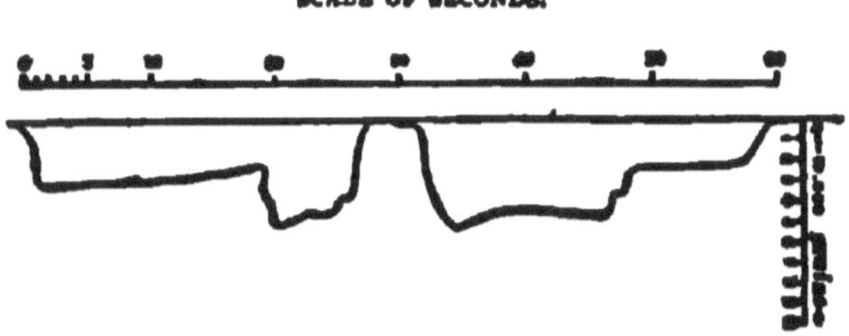

FIG. 12.   DIAGRAM SHOWING TENSION IN CROOKES' APPARATUS UNDER
THE INFLUENCE OF HOME.

stand of the apparatus at P (Fig. 9). A gentleman present
put his hand on Mr. Home's hands, and his foot on
both Mr. Home's feet, and I also watched him
closely all the time.   At the proper moment the clock
was again set going; the board descended and rose in
an irregular manner, the result being a curved tracing
on the glass, of which Fig. 13 is a copy.

SCALE THE SAME AS IN FIG. 12.

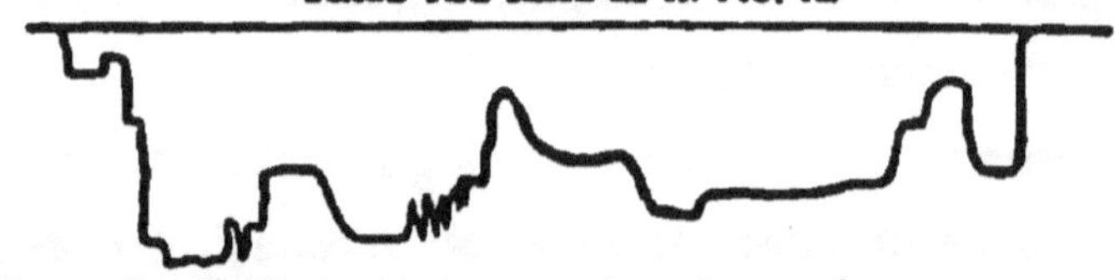

FIG. 13. DIAGRAM SHOWING TENSION IN CROOKES' APPARATUS UNDER THE INFLUENCE OF HOME.

"*Experiment III.*—Mr. Home was now placed one foot from the board, A B, on one side of it. His hands and feet were firmly grasped by a by-stander, and another tracing, of which Fig. 14 is a copy, was taken on the moving glass plate.

SCALE THE SAME AS IN FIG. 12.

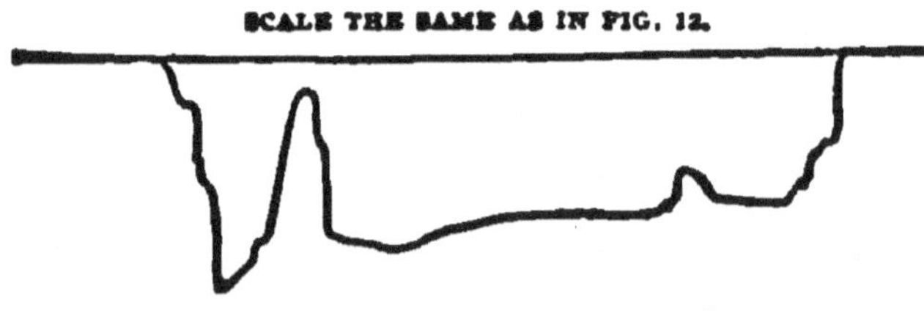

FIG. 14. DIAGRAM SHOWING TENSION IN CROOKES' APPARATUS UNDER HOME'S INFLUENCE.

"*Experiment IV.*—(Tried on an occasion when the power was stronger than on the previous occasions), Mr. Home was now placed 3 feet from the apparatus, his hands and feet being tightly held. The clock was set going when he gave the word, and the end, B,

SCALE THE SAME AS IN FIG. 12.

FIG. 15. DIAGRAM SHOWING TENSION IN CROOKES' APPARATUS UNDER HOME'S INFLUENCE.

of the board soon descended, and again rose in an irregular manner, as shown in Fig. 15.

"The following series of experiments were tried
with more delicate apparatus, and with another person, a lady, Mr. Home being absent. As the lady is
non-professional, I do not mention her name. She
has, however, consented to meet any scientific men
whom I may introduce for purposes of investigation.

"A piece of thin parchment, A, (Figs. 16 and 17), is
stretched tightly across a circular hoop of wood. B
C is a light lever turning on D. At the end B is a
vertical needle point touching the membrane A, and
at C is another needle point, projecting horizontally

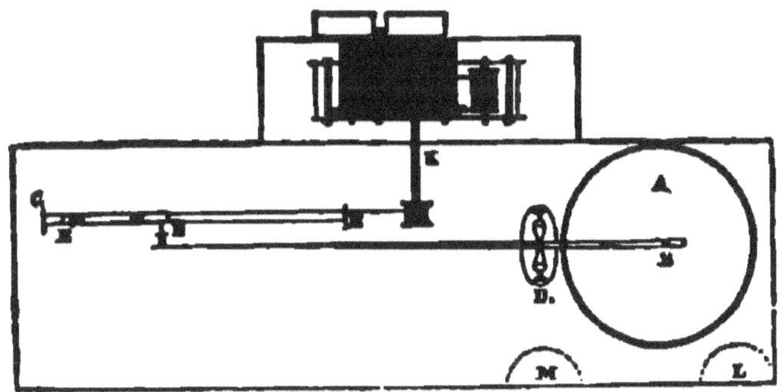

FIG. 16. SECOND CROOKES' APPARATUS.

and touching a smoked glass plate, E F. This
glass plate is drawn along in the direction H G
by clockwork, K. The end, B, of the lever is weighted
so that it shall quickly follow the movements of the

centre of the disc, A. These movements are transmitted and recorded on the glass plate, E F, by means of the lever and needle point, C. Holes are cut in the side of the hoop to allow a free passage of air to the under side of the membrane. The apparatus was well tested beforehand by myself and others, to see that no shaking or jar on the table or support would interfere with the results: the line traced by the point, C,

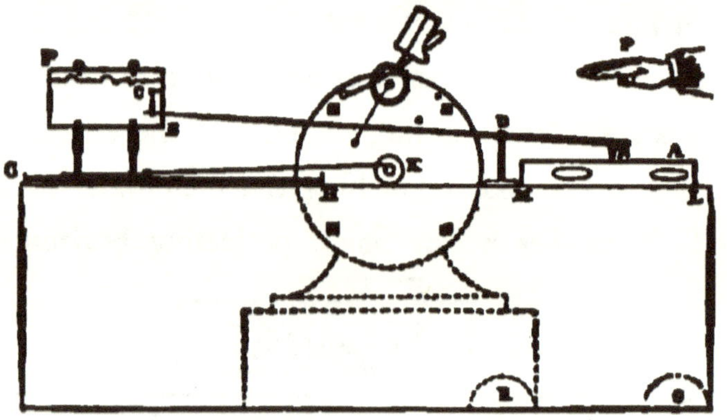

FIG. 17. SECTION OF APPARATUS IN FIG. 16.

on the smoked glass was perfectly straight in spite of all our attempts to influence the lever by shaking the stand or stamping on the floor.

"*Experiment V.*—Without having the object of the instrument explained to her, the lady was brought into the room and asked to place her fingers on the wooden stand at the points, L M, Fig. 16. I then placed my hands over hers to enable me to detect any conscious or unconscious movement on her part. Presently percussive noises were heard on the parchment, resembling the dropping of grains of sand on its surface. At each percussion a fragment of graphite which I had placed on the membrane was seen to be projected upwards about 1-50th of an inch, and the end, C, of the lever moved slightly up and down. Sometimes the sounds were as rapid as those from an induction-coil, whilst at others they were more than a second apart. Five or six tracings were taken, and in all cases a movement of the end, C, of the lever was seen to have occurred with each vibration of the membrane.

"In some cases the lady's hands were not so near the membrane as L M, but were at N O, Fig 17.

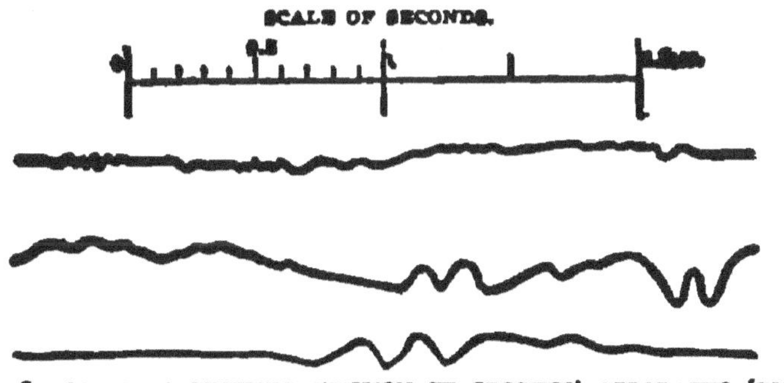

FIG. 18. DIAGRAM SHOWING TENSION IN CROOKES' APPARATUS (FIG. 15 AND 16) OUTSIDE HOME'S INFLUENCE. -

"The accompanying Fig. 18 gives tracings taken from the plates used on these occasions.

"*Experiment VI.*—Having met with these results in Mr. Home's absence, I was anxious to see what action would be produced on the instrument in his presence.

"Accordingly I asked him to try, but without explaining the instrument to him.

"I grasped Mr. Home's right arm above the wrist and held his hand over the membrane, about 10 inches from its surface, in the position shown at P, Fig. 17. His other hand was held by a friend. After remaining in this position for about half a minute, Mr. Home said he felt some influence passing. I then set the clock going, and we all saw the index, C, moving up and down. The movements were much slower than in the former case, and were almost entirely unaccompanied by the percussive vibrations then noticed.

"Figs. 19 and 20 show the curves produced on the glass on two of these occasions.

"Figs. 18, 19 and 20 are magnified.

"These experiments *confirm beyond doubt* the conclusions at which I arrived in my former paper, namely, the existence of a force associated, in some manner not yet explained, with the human organization, by which force increased weight is capable of being imparted to solid bodies without physical contact. In the case of Mr. Home, the development of this force

FIG. 19. DIAGRAM SHOWING TENSION IN CROOKES' APPARATUS (FIG. 16 AND 17) UNDER HOME'S INFLUENCE.

varies enormously, not only from week to week, but from hour to hour; on some occasions the force is inappreciable by my tests for an hour or more, and then suddenly reappears in great strength.

"It is capable of acting at a distance from Mr.

FIG. 20. DIAGRAM SHOWING TENSION IN CROOKES' APPARATUS (FIG. 16 AND 17) UNDER HOME'S INFLUENCE.

Home (not unfrequently as far as two or three feet), but is always strongest close to him.

"Being firmly convinced that there could be no manifestation of one form of force without the corresponding expenditure of some other form of force, I for a long time searched in vain for evidence of any force or power being used up in the production of these results.

"Now, however, having seen more of Mr. Home, I think I perceive what it is that this psychic force uses up for its development. In employing the terms *vital force* or *nervous energy*, I am aware that I am employing words which convey very different significations to many investigators; but after witnessing the painful state of nervous and bodily prostration in which some of these experiments have left Mr. Home —after seeing him lying in an almost fainting condition on the floor, pale and speechless—I could scarcely doubt that the evolution of psychic force is accompanied by a corresponding drain on vital force."

Sergeant Cox in speaking of the tests says, "The results appear to me conclusively to establish the important fact, that there is a force proceeding from the nerve-system capable of imparting motion and weight to solid bodies within the sphere of its influence."

One of the medium's defenders has written:

"Home's mysterious power, whatever it may have been, was very uncertain. Sometimes he could exercise it, and at others not, and these fluctuations were not seldom the source of embarrassment to him. He would often arrive at a place in obedience to an engagement, and, as he imagined, ready to perform, when he would discover himself absolutely helpless. After a séance his exhaustion appeared to be complete.

"There is no more striking proof of the fact that Home really possessed occult gifts of some sort—psychic force or whatever else the power may be termed—than he gave such amazing exhibitions in the early part of his history and was able to do so little toward the end. If it had been juggling he would, like other conjurors, have improved on his tricks by experience, or at all events, while his memory held out he would not have deteriorated."

Dr. Hammond's Experiments,

Dr. William A. Hammond, the eminent neurologist, of Washington, D. C., took up the cudgels against Prof. Crookes' "Psychic Force" theory, and assigned the experiments to the domain of animal electricity. He wrote as follows:* "Place an egg in an egg-cup and balance a long lath upon the egg.

____
*Spiritualism and nervous derangement, New York, 1876. p. 115.

Though the lath be almost a plank it will obediently follow a rod of glass, gutta percha or sealing-wax, which has been previously well dried and rubbed, the former with a piece of silk, and the two latter with woolen cloth. Now, in dry weather, many persons within my knowledge, have only to walk with a shuf-

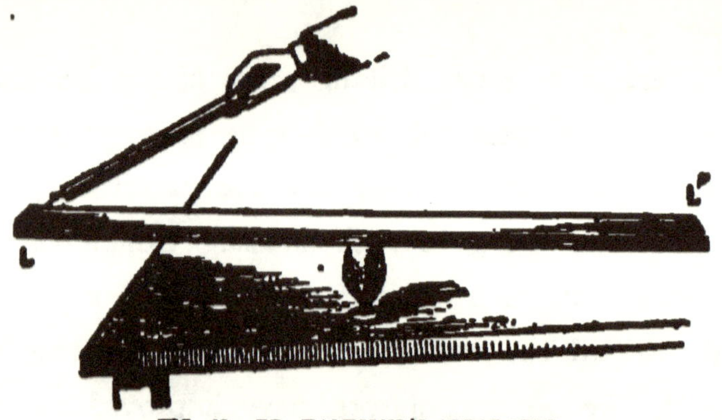

FIG. 21. DR. HAMMOND'S APPARATUS.

fling gait over the carpet, and then approaching the lath hold out the finger instead of the glass, sealing wax or gutta percha, and instantly the end of the lath at L rises to meet it, and the end at L is depressed. Applying these principles, I arranged an apparatus exactly like that of Prof. Crookes, except that the spring balance was such as is used for weighing letters and was therefore very delicate, indicating quarter ounces with exactness, and that the board was thin and narrow.

"Applying the glass rod or stick of sealing-wax to the end resting by its foot on the table, the index of the balance at once descended, showing an increased weight of a little over three quarters of an ounce, and this without the board being raised from the table.

"I then walked over a thick Turkey rug for a few moments, and holding my finger under the board near the end attached to the balance, caused a fall of the index of almost half an ounce. I then rested my finger lightly on the end of the board immediately over the foot, and again the index descended and oscillated several times, just as in Mr. Home's experiments. The lowest point reached was six and a quarter ounces, and as the board weighed, as attached to the balance, five ounces, there was an increased weight of one and a quarter ounces. At no time was the end of the board raised from the table.

"I then arranged the apparatus so as to place a thin glass tumbler nearly full of water immediately over the fulcrum, as in Mr. Crookes' experiment, and again the index fell and oscillated on my fingers being put into the water.

"Now if one person can thus, with a delicate apparatus like mine, cause the index, through electricity, to descend and ascend, it is not improbable that others, like Mr. Home, could show greater, or even different electrical power, as in Prof. Crookes' experiments. It is well known that all persons are not alike in their ability to be electrically excited. Many persons, myself among them, can light the gas with the end of the finger. Others cannot do it with any amount of shuffling over the carpet.

"At any rate is it not much more sensible to believe that Mr. Home's experiments are to be thus explained than to attribute the results of his semi-mysterious attempts to spiritualism or psychic force?"

3. Rope-Tying and Holding Mediums.

THE DAVENPORT BROTHERS.

Ira Erastus and William Henry Davenport were born at Buffalo, N. Y., the former on Sept. 17, 1839, and the latter on February 1, 1841. Their father, Ira Davenport, was in the police detective department, and, it is alleged, invented the celebrated rope-tying feats after having seen the Indian jugglers of the West perform similar illusions. The usual stories about ghostly phenomena attending the childhood of mediums were told about the Davenport Brothers, but it was not until 1855 that they started on their tour of the United States, with their father as showman or spiritual lecturer. When the Civil War broke out, the Brothers, accompanied by Dr. J. B. Ferguson, formerly an Independent minister of Nashville, Tenn., in the capacity of lecturer, and a Mr. Palmer as general agent and manager, went to England to exhibit their mediumistic powers, following the example of D. D. Home. With the company also was a Buffalo boy named Fay, of German-American parentage, who had formerly acted as ticket-taker for the mediums. He discovered the secret of the rope-tying feat, and was an adept at the coat feat, so he was employed as an "under-study" in case of the illness of William Davenport, who was in rather delicate health. The Brothers Davenport at this period, aged respectively 25 and 23 years, had "long black curly hair, broad but not high foreheads, dark eyes, heavy eye-brows and moustaches, firm set lips, and a bright, keen look." Their first performance in England was given at the Concert Rooms, Hanover Square, London, and created intense excitement.

Punch called the *furore* over the spirit rope-tyers the "tie-fuss fever," and said the mediums were "Ministers of the Interior, with a seat in the Cabinet."

J. N. Maskelyne, the London conjurer of Egyptian Hall, wrote of them: "About the Davenport Brothers' performances, I have to say that they were and still remain the most inexplicable ever presented to the public as of spiritual origin; and had they been put forth as feats of jugglery would have awakened a considerable amount of curiosity though certainly not to the extent they did."

In September, 1865, the Brothers arrived in Paris, and placarded the city with enormous posters announcing that the Brothers Davenport, spirit-mediums, would give a series of public séances at the *Salle Hers*. Their reputation had preceded them to France and the *boulevardiers* talked of nothing but the wonderful American mediums and their mysterious cabinet. Before exhibiting in Paris the Davenports visited the *Chateau de Gennevilliers*, whose owner was an enthusiastic believer in Spiritism, and gave a séance before a select party of journalists and scientific men. The exhibition was pronounced marvellous in the extreme and perfectly inexplicable.

The Parisian press was divided on the subject of the Davenports and their advertised séances. Some of the papers protested against such performances on the ground that they were dangerous to the mental health of the public, and, one writer said, "Particularly to those weaker intellects which are always ready enough to accept as gospel the tricks and artifices of the adepts of sham witchcraft." M. Edmond About, the famous journalist and novelist, in the *Opinion Nationale*, wrote a scathing denunciation of Spiritism, but all to no purpose, except to inflame public curiosity.

The performances of the Davenports were divided into two parts: (1) The light séance, (2) the dark séance. In the light séance a cabinet, elevated from the stage by three trestles, was used. It was a simple wooden structure with three doors. In the centre door was a lozenge-shaped window covered with a curtain. Upon the sides of the cabinet hung various musical instruments, a guitar, a violin, horns, tambourines, and a big dinner bell.

A committee chosen by the audience tied the mediums' hands securely behind their backs, fastened their legs together, and pinioned them to their seats in the cabinet, and to the cross rails with strong ropes. The side doors were closed first, then the center door, but no sooner was the last fastened, than the hands of one of the mediums were thrust through

FIG. 22. THE DAVENPORT BROTHERS IN THEIR CABINET.

thewindow in the centre door. In a very short time,at asignalfrom the mediums, the doors were opened,and the Davenports stepped forth, with the ropes in their hands, every knot untied, confessedly by spirit power. The astonishment of the spectators amounted to awe. On an average it took ten minutes to pinion the Brothers; but a single minute was required for their release. Once more the mediums went into the cabinet, this time with the ropes lying in a coil at their feet. Two minutes elapsed. Hey, presto! the doors were opened, and the Davenports were pronounced by the committee to be securely lashed to their seats. Seals were affixed to the knots in the ropes, and the doors closed as before. Pandemonium reigned. Bells were rung, horns blown, tambourines thumped, violins played, and guitars vigorously twanged. Heavy rappings also were heard on the ceiling, sides and floor of the cabinet, then after a brief but absolute silence, a bare hand and arm emerged from the lozenge window, and rung the big dinner bell. On opening the doors the Brothers were found securely tied as before, and seals intact. An amusing feature of the exhibition occurred when a venturesome spectator volunteered to sit inside of the cabinet between the two mediums. He came out with his coat turned inside out and his hat jammed over his eyes. In the dark séance the cabinet was dispensed with and the spectators, holding hands, formed a ring around the mediums. The lights were put out and similar phenomena took place, with the addition of luminous hands, and musical instruments floating in the air.

Robert-Houdin wrote an interesting brochure on the Davenports, ("Secrets of Stage Conjuring," translated by Prof. Hoffmann) from which I take the following: "The ropes used by the Davenport Brothers are of a cotton fibre; and they present therefore smooth surfaces, adapted to slip easily one upon another. Gentlemen are summoned from the audience to tie the mediums. Now, tell me, is it an easy task for an amateur to tie a man up off-hand with a rope three yards long, in a very secure way? The amateur is flurried, self-conscious, anxious to acquit himself well of the business, but he is a gentleman, not a brute, and if one of the Brothers sees the ropes getting into a dangerous tangle, he gives a slight groan, as if he were being injured, and the instantaneous impulse of the other man is to loosen the cord a trifle. A fraction of an inch is an invaluable gain in the after-business of loosening the ropes. Sometimes the stiffening of a muscle, the raising of a shoulder, the crooking of a knee, gives all the play required by the Brothers in ridding themselves of their bonds. Their muscles and joints are wonderfully supple, too; the thumbs can be laid flat in the palm of the hand, the hand itself rounded until it is no broader than the wrist, and then it is easy to pull through. Violent wrenches send the ropes up toward the shoulder, vigorous shakings get the legs free; the first hand untied is thrust through the hole in the door of the cabinet, and then returns to give aid to more serious knots on his own or his brother's person. In tying themselves up the Davenports used the slip-knot, a sort of bow, the ends of which have only to be pulled to be tightened or loosened."

This slip-knot is a very ingenious affair. (See Fig. 23.) In performing the spirit-tying, the mediums went into the cabinet with the ropes examined by the audience lying coiled at their feet. The doors were closed. They had concealed about their persons ropes in which these trick knots were already adjusted, and with which they very speedily secured themselves, having first secreted the genuine ropes.

Then the doors were opened. Seals were affixed to the knots, but this sealing, owing to the position of the hands, and the careful exposition of the knots did not affect the slipping of the ropes suf- ficiently to prevent the mediums from removing and replacing their hands.

NO. 23. TRICK-TIE USED IN CABINET WORK.

In the dark séance, flour was sometimes placed in the pinioned hands of the Davenports. On being re- leased from their bonds, the flour was found undis- turbed.

This was considered a convincing test; for how could the Brothers possibly manipulate the musical instruments with their hands full of flour. One day a wag substituted a handful of snuff for flour, and when the mediums were examined, the snuff had disap- peared and flour taken its place. As will be understood, in the above test the Davenports emptied the flour from their hands into secret pockets and at the proper moment took out cornucopias of flour and filled their hands again before securing themselves in the famous slip-knots.

Among the exposés of the Brothers Davenport, Herrmann, the conjurer, gives the following in the *Cosmopolitan Magazine:* "The Davenports, for thirteen years, in Europe and America, augmented the faith in Spiritualism. Unfortunately for the Davenports they appeared at Ithaca, New York, where is situated Cornell University. The students having a scientific trend of mind, provided themselves before attending the performance with pyrotechnic balls containing phosphorus, so made as to ignite suddenly with a bright light. During the dark séance when the Davenports were supposed to be bound hand and foot within the closet and when the guitars were apparently floating in the air, the students struck their lights, whereupon the spirits were found to be no other than the Davenports themselves, dodging about the stage brandishing guitars and playing tunes and waving at the same time tall poles surmounted by phosphorescent spook pictures."

The Davenports had some stormy experiences in Paris, but managed to come through all successfully, with plenty of French gold in their pockets. William died in October, 1877, at the Oxford Hotel, Sydney, Australia, having publicly denounced Spiritualism. Mr. Fay took to raising sheep in Australia, while Ira Davenport drifted back to his old home in Buffalo, New York.

Many mediums, taking the cue from the Davenports, have performed the cabinet act with its accompanying rope-tying, but the conjurers (anti-spiritists) have, with the aid of mechanism, brought the business to a high degree of perfection, notably Mr. J. Nevil Maskelyne, of Egyptian Hall, London, and Mr. Harry Kellar, of the United States. Writing of the Davenport Brothers, Maskelyne says:

"The instantaneous tying and untying was simply marvellous, and it utterly baffled everyone to discover, until, on one occasion, the accidental falling of a piece of drapery from a window (the lozenge-shaped aperture in the door of the cabinet), at a critical moment let me into the secret. I was able in a few months to reproduce every item of the Davenports' cabinet and dark séance. So close was the resemblance to the original, that *the Spiritualist had no alternative but to claim us* (Maskelyne and Cooke) *as most powerful spirit mediums who found it more profitable to deny the assistance of spirits.*"

Robert-Houdin's explanation of the slip-knot, used by the Davenports in their dark séance, is the correct one, but he failed to fathom the mystery of the mode of release of the Brothers after they were tied in the cabinet by a committee selected from the audience. Anyone trying to extricate himself from bondage *a la* Houdin, no matter how slippery and serpentine he be, would find it exceedingly difficult. It seems almost incredible, but trickery was used in the light séance, as well as the dark. Maskelyne, as quoted above, claimed to have penetrated the mystery, but he kept it a profound secret—though he declared that his cabinet work was trickery. The writer is indebted for an initiation into the mysteries of the Davenport Brothers' rope-tying to Mr. H. Morgan Robinson (Professor Helmann), of Washington, D. C., a very clever prestidigitateur.

In the year 1895, after an unbroken silence of nineteen years, Fay, ex-assistant of the Davenports, determined to resume the profession of public medium.

He abandoned his sheep ranch and hunted up Ira
Davenport. They gave several performances in
Northern towns, and finally landed at the Capital of
the Nation, in the spring of 1895, and advertised several séances at Willard's Hall. A very small audience greeted them on their first appearance. Among
the committee volunteering to go on the stage and
tie the mediums were the writer and Mr. Robinson.
After the séance the prestidigitateur fully explained the
modus operandi of the mystic tie, which is herein for
the first time correctly given to the public.

The medium holds out his left wrist first and has
it tied securely, about the middle of the rope. Two
members of the committee are directed to pull the
ends of the cord vigorously. "Are you confident that
the knots are securely tied?" he asks; when the committee respond "yes," he puts his hand quickly behind
him, and places against the wrist, the wrist of his
right hand, in order that they may be pinioned together During this rapid movement he twists the
rope about the knot on his left wrist, thereby allowing
enough slack cord to disengage his right hand when
necessary. To slip the right hand back into place is
an easy matter. After both hands are presumably

tied, the medium steps into the cabinet; the ends of the rope are pushed through two holes in the chair or wooden seat, by the committee and made fast to the medium's legs. Bells ring, horns blow, and the performer's hand is thrust through the window of the cabinet. Finally a gentleman is requested to enter the cabinet with the medium. The doors are locked and a perfect pandemonium begins; when they are opened the volunteer assistant tumbles out in great trepidation. His hat is smashed over his eyes, his cravat is tied around his leg, and he is found to have on the medium's coat, while the medium wears the gentleman's coat turned inside out. It all appears very remarkable, but the mystery is cleared up when I state that the innocent looking gentleman is invariably a confederate, what conjurers call a *plant*, because he is planted in the audience to volunteer for the special act.

Ira and William Davenport were tied in the manner above described. Often one of the Brothers allowed himself to be genuinely pinioned, after having received a preconcerted signal from his partner that all was right. *i. e.*, the partner had been fastened by the trick tie, calling attention to the knots in the cord, etc. The trick tic, however, is so delusive, that it is impossible to penetrate the secret in the short time allowed the committee for investigation, and there is no special reason for permitting a genuine tie-up. Once in a great while, the Davenports were over-reached by clever committee-men and tied up so tightly that there was no getting loose. Where one brother failed to execute the trick and was genuinely fastened, the other medium performed the spirit evolutions, and cut his "confrere" loose before they came out of the cabinet.

The Fay-Davenport revival proved a failure, and the mediums dissolved partnership in Washington. Kellar, the magician and former assistant of the original Davenport combination, by a curious coincidence was giving his fine conjuring exhibition in the city at the same time. His tricks far eclipsed the feeble revival of the rope-tying phenomena. The fickle public crowded to see the magician and neglected the mediums.

ANNIE EVA FAY.

One of the most famous of the materializing mediums now exhibiting in the United States is Annie

Eva Fay. She is quite an adept at the spirit-tying business, and like the Davenports, uses a cabinet on the stage, but her method of tying, though clever, is inferior to that used by the Brothers in their balmy days. In the center of the Fay cabinet (a plain, cur- . tained affair) is a post firmly screwed to the stage. The medium permits a committee of two from the audience to tie her to this post, and seal the bandages about her wrists with court plaster. She then takes her seat upon a small stool in front of the stanchion; the musical instruments are placed on her lap, and the curtains of the cabinet closed. Immediately the evidences of *spirit power* begin: the bell is jingled, the tambourine thumped, and the sound of a horn heard, simultaneously.

The Fay method of tying is designed especially to facilitate the medium's actions. Cotton bandages are used, and the committee are invited to sew the knots through and through. Each wrist is tied with a bandage, about an inch and a half wide by a half yard in length; and the medium then clasps her hands behind her, so that her wrists are about six inches apart. The committee now proceed to tie the ends of the bandages firmly together, and, after this is accomplished, the dangling pieces of the bandages are clipped off. It is true, the medium is firmly bound by this process, and it would be physically impossible for her to release herself, without disturbing the sewing and the seals, but it is not intended for her to release herself at all; the method pursued being altogether different from the old species of rope-tying. All being secure, the committee are requested to pass another bandage about the short ligature between the lady's wrists, and tie it in double square knots, and firmly secure this to a ring in the post of the cabinet, the medium being seated on a stool in front of the stanchion, facing the audience. Her neck is likewise secured to the post by cotton bandages and her feet fastened together with a cord, the end of which passes out of the cabinet and is held by one of the committee.

The peculiar manner of holding the hands, described above, enables the medium to secure for her use, a ligature of knotted cloth between her hands, some six inches long; and the central bandage, usually tied in four or five double knots, gives her about two inches play between the middle of the cotton handcuffs and the ring in the post, to which it is secured. The ring is two and a half inches in diameter, and the staple which holds it to the stanchion is a half inch. The left hand of the medium gives six additional inches, and the bandage on her wrist slips readily along her slender arm nearly half way to the elbow—"all of which," says John W. Truesdell,* who was the first to expose Miss Fay's spirit pretensions, "gives the spirits a clear leeway of not less than 20 inches from the stanchion. The moment the curtain is closed, the medium, under spirit influence spreads her hands as far apart as possible, an act which stretches the knotted ligature so that the bandage about it will easily slip from the centre to either wrist; then, throwing her lithe form by a quick movement, to the left, so that her hips will pass the stanchion without moving her feet from the floor, the spirits are able, through the medium, to reach whatever may have been placed upon her lap."

One of Annie Eva's most convincing tests is the accordion which plays, after it has been bound fast with tapes and the tapes carefully sealed at every note, so as to prevent its being performed on in the regular manner. Her method of operating, though

---

*The Bottom Facts Concerning the Science of Spiritualism, etc., New York, 1883.

simple, is decidedly ingenious. She places a small tube in the valve-hole of the instrument, breathes and blows alternately into it, and then by fingering the keys, executes an air with excellent effect.

Sometimes she places a musical box on an oblong plate of glass suspended from the ceiling by four cords. The box plays and stops at word of command, much to the astonishment of listeners. "Electricity," exclaims the reader! Hardly so, for the box is completely insulated on the sheet of glass. Then how is it done? Mr. Arprey Vere, an investigator of spirit phenomena, tells the secret in the following words: ("Modern Magic"). "In the box there is placed a balance lever which when the glass is in the slightest degree tilted, arrests the fly-fan, and thus prevents the machinery from moving. At the word of command the glass is made level, and the fly-fan being released, the machinery moves, and a tune is played. When commanded to stop, either side of the cord is pulled by a confederate behind the scenes, the balance lever drops, the fly-fan is arrested, and the music stops."

One of the tests presented to the American public by this medium is the "spirit-hand," constructed of painted wood or *papier mache*, which raps out answers to questions, after it has been isolated from all contact by being placed on a sheet of glass supported on the backs of two chairs.

It is a trick performed by every conjurer, and the secret is a piece of black silk thread, worked by confederates stationed in the wings of the theatre, one at the right, the other at the left. The thread lies along the stage when not in use, but at the proper cue from the medium, it is lifted up and brought in contact with the wooden hand. The hand is so constructed that the palm lies on the glass sheet and the wrist, with a fancy lace cuff about it, is elevated an inch above the glass, the whole apparatus being so pivoted that a pressure of the thread from above will depress the wrist and elevate the palm. When the thread is relaxed the hand comes down on the glass with a thump and makes the spirit rap which is so effective. A rapping skull made on similar principles is also in vogue among mediums.

CHARLES SLADE.

Annie Eva Fay has a rival in Charles Slade, who is a clever performer and a most convincing talker. His cabinet test is the same as Miss Fay's, but he has other specialties that are worth explaining—one is the "table-raising," and another is the "spirit neck-tie." The effect of the first experiment is as fol-lows: Slade, with his arms bared and coat removed, requests several gentlemen to sit around a long table, reserving the head for himself. Hands are placed on the table, and developments awaited. "Do you feel the table raising?" asks the medium, after a short pause. "We do!" comes the response of the sitters. Slade then rises; all stand up, and the table is seen suspended in the air, about a foot from the floor of the stage. In a little while an uncontrollable desire seems to take possession of the table to rush about the stage. Frequently the medium requests several persons to get on the table, but that has no effect whatever. The same levitation takes place. The se-cret of this surprising mediumistic test is very simple. In the first place, the man who sits at the foot of the table is a confederate. Both medium and confeder-ate wear about their waists wide leather belts, ribbed and strengthened with steel bands, and supported from the shoulders by bands of leather and steel. In the front of each belt is a steel hinge concealed by the vest of the wearer. In the act of sitting down at the table the medium and his confederate quickly pull the hinges which catch under the top of the table when the sitters rise. The rest of the trick is easily comprehended. When the levitation act is finished the hinges are folded up and hidden under the vests of the performers.

The "spirit neck-tie" is one of the best things in the whole range of mediumistic marvels, and has never to my knowledge been exposed. A rope is tied about the medium's neck with the knots at the back and the ends are thrust through two holes in one side of the cabinet, and tied in a bow knot on the outside. The holes in the cabinet must be on a level with the medium's neck, after he is seated. The curtains of the cabinet are then closed, and the committee requested to keep close watch on the bow-knot on the outside of the cabinet: The assistant in a short time pulls back the curtain from the cabinet on the side farthest from the medium, and reveals a sheeted figure which writes messages and speaks to the spectators. Other materializations take place. The curtain is drawn. At this juncture the medium is heard calling: "Quick, quick, release me!" The assistant unfastens the bow-knot, the ends of the rope are quickly drawn into the cabinet, and the medium comes forward, looking somewhat exhausted, with the rope still tied about his neck. The question resolves itself into two factors—either the medium gets loose the neck-tie and impersonates the spirits or the materializations are genuine. "Gets loose! But that is impossible," exclaim the committee, "we watched the cord in the closest way." The secret of this surprising feat lies in a clever substitution. The tie is genuine, but the medium, after the curtains of the cabinet are closed, cuts the cord with a sharp knife, just about the region of the throat, and impersonates the ghosts, with the aid of various wigs and disguises concealed about him. Then he takes a second cord from his pocket, ties it about his neck with the same number of knots as are in the original rope and twists the neck-tie around so that these knots will appear at the back of his neck. Now, he exclaims, "Quick, quick, unfasten the cord." As soon as his assistant has untied the simple bow knot on the outside of the cabinet, the medium quickly pulls the genuine rope into the cabinet and conceals it in his pocket.

When he presents himself to the spectators the rope

SLADE

Will fully demonstrate the various methods employed by such renowned spiritualistic mediums as Alex. Hume, Mrs.
Hoffmann, Prof. Taylor, Chas. Cooke,
Richard Bishop, Dr. Arnold, and various
others,

IN PLAIN, OPEN LIGHT.

Every possible means will be used to enlighten the auditor
as to whether these so-called wonders are enacted through the
aid of spirits or are the result of natural agencies.

SUCH PHENOMENA AS

Spirit Materializations,
  Marvelous Superhuman Visions,
    Spiritualistic Rappings,
      Slate Writing,
        Spirit Pictures,
          Floating Tables and Chairs,
            Remarkable Test of the Human Mind,
            Second Sight Mysteries,
A Human Being Isolated from Surrounding Objects
            Floating in Mid-Air.

Committees will be selected by the audience to assist
SLADE, and to report their views as to the why and wherefore
of the many strange things that will be shown during the evening. This is done so that every person attending may learn
the truth regarding the tests, whether they are genuine, or
caused by expert trickery.

Do not class or confound SLADE with the numerous so-
called spirit mediums and spiritual exposers that travel through
the country, like a set of roaming vampires, seeking whom
they may devour. It is SLADE'S object in coming to your
city to enlighten the people one way or the other as to the real

TRUTH CONCERNING THESE MYSTERIES.

Scientific men, and many great men, have believed there was a grain of essential truth in the claims of Spiritualism. It was believed more on the account of the want of power to deny it than anything else. The idea that under some strained and indefinable possibilities the spirit of the mortal man may communicate with the spirit of the departed man is something that the great heart of humanity is prone to believe, as it has faith in future existence No skeptic will deny any man's right to such a belief, but this little grain of hope has been the foundation for such extensive and heartless mediumistic frauds that it is constantly losing ground.

A NIGHT OF

Wonderful Manifestations

THE VEIL DRAWN

So that all may have an insight into the

SPIRIT WORLD

And behold many things that are

Strange and Startling.

The Clergy, the Press, Learned Synods and Councils, Sage Philosophers and Scientists, in fact, the whole world have proclaimed these Philosophical Idealisms to be an astounding

FACT.

YOU ARE BROUGHT

Face to Face with the Spirits.

A SMALL ADMISSION WILL BE CHARGED TO DEFRAY EXPENSES.

about his neck (presumed to be the original) is found to be correctly tied and untampered with. Much of the effect depends on the rapidity with which the medium conceals the original cord and comes out of the cabinet. The author has seen this trick performed in parlors, the holes being bored in a door.

Charles Slade makes a great parade in his advertisements about exposing the vulgar tricks of bogus mediums, but he says nothing about the secrets of his own pet illusions. His exposés are made for the purpose of enhancing his own mediumistic marvels.

I insert a verbatim copy of the handbills with which he deluges the highways and byways of American cities and towns.

PIERRE L. O. A. KEELER.

Pierre Keeler's fame as a producer of spirit phenomena rests largely upon his materializing séances. It was his materializations that received the particular attention of the Seybert Commission. The late Mr. Henry Seybert, who was an ardent believer in modern Spiritualism, presented to the University of Pennsylvania a sum of money to found a chair of philosophy, with the proviso that the University should appoint a commission to investigate "all systems of morals, religion or philosophy which assume to represent the truth, and particularly of modern Spiritualism." The following gentlemen were accordingly appointed, and began their investigations: Dr. William Pepper, Dr. Joseph Leidy, Dr. George A. Koenig, Prof. R. E. Thompson, Prof. George S. Fullerton, and Dr. Horace H. Furness. Subsequently others were added to the commission—Dr. Coleman Sellers, Dr. James W. White, Dr. Calvin B. Kneer, and Dr. S. Weir Mitchell. Dr. Pepper, Provost of the University, was *ex-officio* chairman; Dr. Furness, acting chairman, and Prof. Fullerton, secretary.

Keeler's materializations are thus described in the report of the commission:

"On May 27 the Seybert commission held a meeting at the house of Mr. Furness at 8 p. m., to examine the phenomena occurring in the presence of Mr. Pierre L. O. A. Keeler, a professional medium.

"The medium, Mr. Keeler, is a young man, with well cut features, curly brown hair, a small sandy mustache, and rather worn and anxious expression;

he is strongly built, about 5 feet 8 inches high, and
with rather short, quite broad, and very muscular
hands and strong wrists. The hands were examined
by Dr. Pepper and Mr. Fullerton after the séance.

"The séance was held in Mr. Furness' drawing-
room, and a space was curtained off by the medium
in the northeast corner, thus, (Fig. 25):

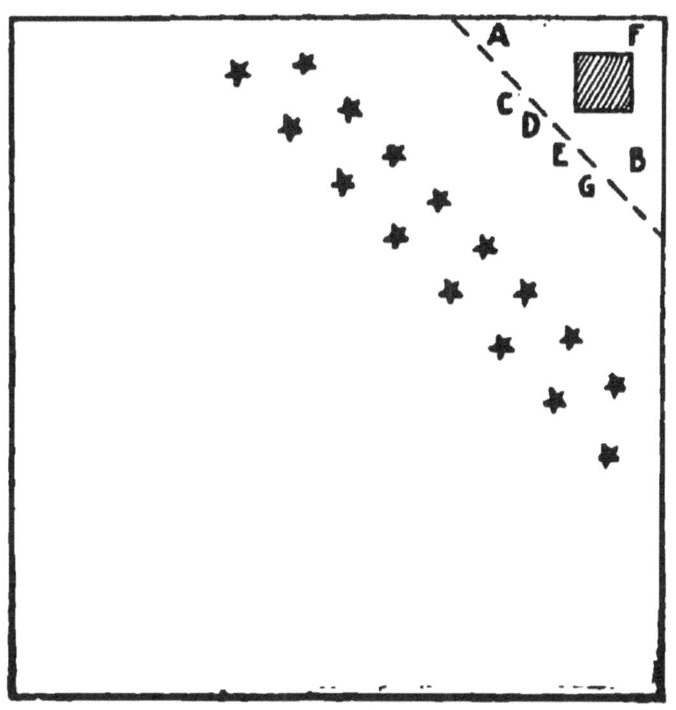

FIG. 25. PIERRE KEELER'S CABINET SEANCE.

"The curtain is represented by A, B; C, D and E
are three chairs, placed in front of the curtain by the

medium, in one of which (E) he afterwards sat; G denotes the position of Mrs. Keeler; F is a small table, placed within the curtain, and upon which was a tambourine, a guitar, two bells, a hammer, a metallic ring; the stars show the positions of the spectators, who sat in a double row—the two stars at the top facing the letter A indicate the positions taken by Mrs. Kase and Col. Kase, friends of Mr. Keeler, according to the directions of the medium.

"The curtain, or rather curtains, were of black muslin, and arranged as follows: There was a plain black curtain, which was stretched across the corner, falling to the floor. Its height, when in position, was 53 inches; it was made thus:

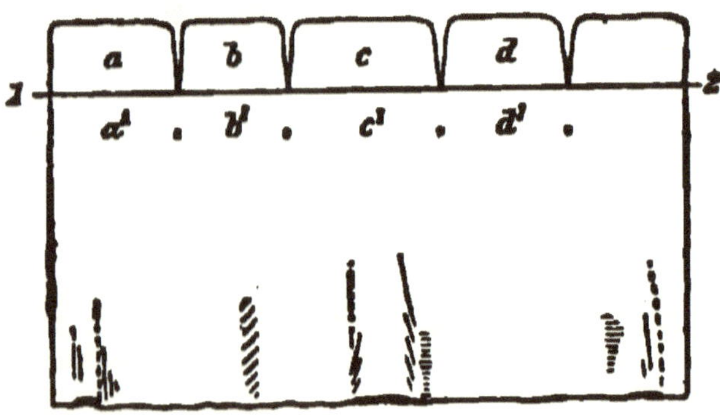

FIG. 26. PIERRE KEELER'S CABINET CURTAIN.

"The cord which held the curtain was 1, 2, and the flaps which are represented as standing above it (A,

B, C, etc.), fell down over A1, B1, C1, etc., and could be made to cover the shoulders of one sitting with his back against the curtain. A black curtain was also pinned against the wall, in the space curtained off, partly covering it. Another curtain was added to the one pictured, as will be described presently.

"The medium asked Col. Kase to say a few words as to the necessity of observing the conditions, need of harmony, etc. And then the medium himself spoke a few words of similar import. He then drew the curtain along the cord (1, 2,) and fastened it; placed three wooden chairs in front of the curtain, as indicated in the diagram, and, saying he needed to form a battery, asked Miss Agnes Irwin to sit in chair D, and Mr. Yost in chair C, the medium himself sitting in chair E. A black curtain was then fastened by Mrs. Keeler over Mr. Keeler, Miss Irwin and Mr. Yost, being fastened at G, between E and D, between D and C, and beyond A; thus entirely covering the three sitting in front of the stretched curtain up to their necks; and when the flaps before mentioned were pulled down over their shoulders, nothing could be seen but the head of each.

"Before the last curtain was fastened over them,

the medium placed both his hands upon the forearm and wrist of Miss Irwin, the sleeve being pulled up for the purpose, and Miss Irwin grasped with her right hand the left wrist of Mr. Yost, his right hand being in sight to the right of the curtain.

"After some piano music the medium said he felt no power from this 'battery,' and asked Mrs. E. D. Gillespie to take Miss Irwin's place. Hands and curtains were arranged as before. The lights were turned down until the room was quite dim. During the singing the medium turned to speak to Mr. Yost, and his body, which had before faced rather away from the two other persons of the 'battery' (which position would have brought his right arm out in front of the stretched curtain), was now turned the other way, so that had he released his grasp upon Mrs. Gillespie's arm, his own right arm could have had free play in the curtained space behind him. His left knee also no longer stood out under the curtain in front, but showed a change of position.

"At this time Mrs. Gillespie declared she felt a touch, and soon after so did Mr. Yost. The medium's body was distinctly inclined toward Mr. Yost at this time. Mrs. Gillespie said she felt taps, but declared that, to the best of her knowledge, she still felt the medium's two hands upon her arm.

"Raps indicated that the spirit, George Christy, was present. As one of those present played on the piano, the tambourine was played in the curtained space and thrown over the curtain; bells were rung; the guitar was thrummed a little. At this time the medium's face was toward Mrs. Gillespie, and his right side toward the curtain. His body was further in against the curtain than either of the others. Upon being asked, Mrs. Gillespie then said she thought she still felt two hands upon her arm.

"The guitar was then thrust out, at least the end of it was, at the bottom of the curtain, between Mrs. Gillespie and the medium. Mrs. Keeler drawing the curtain from over the toes of the medium's boots, to show where his feet were; the guitar was thrummed a little. Had the medium's right arm been free the thrumming could have been done quite easily with one hand. Afterward the guitar was elevated above the curtain; the tambourine, which was by Mrs. Keeler placed upon a stick held up within the inclosure, was made to whirl by the motion of the stick.

The phenomena occurred successively, not simultaneously.

"When the guitar was held up, and when the tambourine was made to whirl, both of these were to the right of the medium, chiefly behind Mrs. Gillespie; they were just where they might have been produced by the right arm of the medium, had it been free. Two clothes-pins were then passed over the curtain, and they were used in drumming to piano music. They could easily be used in drumming by one hand alone, the fingers being thrust into them. The pins were afterward thrown out over the curtain. Mr. Sellers picked one up as soon as it fell, and found it warm in the split, as though it had been worn. The drumming was probably upon the tambourine.

"A hand was seen moving rapidly with a trembling motion—which prevented it from being clearly observed—above the back curtain, between Mr. Yost and Mrs. Gillespie. Paper was passed over the curtain into the cabinet and notes were soon thrown out. The notes could have been written upon the small table within the enclosure by the right hand of the medium, had it been free. Mrs. Keeler then passed a coat over the curtain, and an arm was passed through the sleeve, the fingers, with the cuff around them being shown over the curtain. They were kept moving, and a close scrutiny was not possible.

"Mr. Furness was then invited to hold a writing tablet in front of the curtain, when the hand, almost concealed by the coat-sleeve and the flaps mentioned as attached to the curtain, wrote with a pencil on the tablet. The writing was rapid, and the hand, when not writing, was kept in constant, tremulous motion. The hand was put forth, in this case not over the top curtain, but came from under the flap, and could easily have been the medium's right hand were it disengaged, for it was about on a level with his shoulder and to his right, between him and Mrs. Gillespie. Mr. Furness was allowed to pass his hand close to the curtain and grasp the hand for a moment. It was a right hand.

"Soon after the medium complained of fatigue, and the sitting was discontinued. It was declared by the Spiritualists present to be a fairly successful séance. When the curtains were removed the small table in the enclosure was found to be overturned, and the bells, hammer, etc., on the floor.

"It is interesting to note the space within which all the manifestations occurred. They were, without exception, where they would have been had they been produced by the medium's right arm. Nothing happened to the left of the medium, nor very far over to the right. The sphere of activity was between the medium and Mr. Yost, and most of the phenomena occurred, as, for example, the whirling of the tambourine, behind Mrs. Gillespie.

"The front curtain—that is, the main curtain which hung across the corner—was 85 inches in length, and the cord which supported it 53 inches from the floor. The three chairs which were placed in front of it were side by side, and it would not have been difficult for the medium to reach across and touch Mr. Yost. When Mrs. Keeler passed objects over the curtain, she invariably passed them to the right of the medium, although her position was on his left; and the clothes-pins, paper, pencil, etc., were all passed over at a point where the medium's right hand could easily have reached them.

"To have produced the phenomena by using his right hand the medium would have had to pass it under the curtain at his back. This curtain was not quite hidden by the front one at the end, near the medium, and this end both Mr. Sellers and Dr. Pepper saw rise at the beginning of the séance. The only thing worthy of consideration, as opposed to a natural explanation of the phenomena, was the grasp of the medium's hand on Mrs. Gillespie's arm.

"The grasp was evidently a tight one above the wrist, for the arm was bruised for about four inches. There was no evidence of a similar pressure above that, as the marks on the arm extended in all about five or six inches only. The pressure was sufficient to destroy the sensibility of the forearm, and it is doubtful whether Mrs. Gillespie, with her arm in such a condition could distinguish between the grasp of one hand, with a divided pressure (applied by the two last fingers and the thumb and index) and a double grip by two hands. Three of our number, Mr. Sellers, Mr. Furness, and Dr. White, can, with one hand, perfectly simulate the double grip.

"It is specially worthy of note that Mrs. Gillespie declared that, when the medium first laid hold of her arms with his right hand before the curtain was put over them, it was with an undergrip, and she felt his right arm under her left. But when the medium asked her if she felt both his hands upon her arm, and she said, yes, she could feel the grasp, but no arm under hers, though she moved her elbow around to find it—she felt a hand, but not an arm, and at no time during the séance did she find that arm.

"It should be noted that both the medium and Mr. Yost took off their coats before being covered with the curtain. It was suggested by Dr. Pepper that this might have been required by the medium as a precaution against movements on the part of Mr. Yost. The white shirt-sleeves would have shown against the black background."

I attended a number of Keeler's materializing exhibitions in Washington, D. C., in the spring of 1895, and it is my opinion that the writing of his so-called spirit messages is a simple affair, the very long and elaborate ones being written before the séance begins and the short ones by the medium during the sitting. The latter are done in a scrawling, uncertain hand, just such penmanship one would execute when blindfolded.

The evidence of Dr. G. H. La Fetra, of Washington, D. C., is sufficiently convincing on this point. Said Dr. La Fetra to me: "Some years ago I went with a friend,

Col. Edward Hayes, to one of Mr. Keeler's light seances. It was rather early in the evening, and but few persons had assembled. Upon the mantel piece of the seance-room were several tablets of paper. Unobserved, I took up these tablets, one at a time, and drew the blade of my pen-knife across one end of each of them, so that I might identify the slips of paper torn therefrom by the nicks in them. In a little while, the room was filled with people, and the seance began; the gas being lowered to a dim religious light. When the time came for the writing, Mr. Keeler requested that some of the tablets of paper on the mantel be passed into the cabinet. This was done. Various persons present received 'spirit' communications, the slips of paper being thrown over the curtain of the cabinet by a 'materialized' hand. Some gentleman picked up the papers and read them, for the benefit of the spectators; afterwards he laid aside those not claimed by anybody. Some of these 'spirit' communications covered almost an entire slip. These were carefully written, some o' them in a fine hand. The short messages were roughly scrawled. After the seance, Col. Hayes and myself quietly pocketed a dozen or more of the slips. The next morning at my office we carefully examined them. In every instance, we found that the well-written, lengthy messages were inscribed on *unnicked* slips, the short ones being written on *nicked* slips."

To me, this evidence of Dr. La Fetra seems most conclusive, proving beyond the shadow of a doubt that Keeler prepared his long communications before the séance and had them concealed upon his person, throwing them out of the cabinet at the proper moment. He used the *nicked* tablets for his short messages, written on the spot, thereby completely revealing his method of operating to the ingenious investigator.

The late Dr. Leonard Caughey, of Baltimore, Maryland, an intimate friend of the writer, made a specialty of anti-Spiritualistic tricks, and among others performed this cabinet test of Keeler's. He bought the secret from a broken-down medium for a few dollars, and added to it certain effects of his own, that far surpassed any of Keeler's. The writer has seen Dr. Caughey give the tests, and create the utmost astonishment. His improvement on the trick consisted in the use of a spring clasp like those used by gentlemen bicycle riders to keep their trousers in at the ankles. One end terminated in a soft rubber or chamois skin tip, shaped like a thumb, the other end had four representations of fingers. Two wire rings were soldered on the back of the clasp. This apparatus he had concealed under his vest. Before the curtain of the cabinet was drawn, Dr. Caughey grasped the arm of the lady on his right in the following manner: The thumb of his left hand under her wrist, the fingers extended above it; the thumb of his right hand restin_ on the thumb of the left, the fingers lightly resting on the fingers of the left hand. As soon as the curtain was fastened he extended the fourth and index fingers of the left hand to the fullest extent and pressed hard upon the lady's arm, relaxing at the same time the pressure of his second and third fingers. This movement exactly simulates the grasp of two hands, and enables the medium to take away his right hand altogether. Dr. Caughey then took his spring clasp, opened it by inserting his thumb and first finger in the soldered rings above mentioned, and lightly fastened it on the lady's arm near the wrist, relaxing the pressure of the first and fourth fingers of the left hand at the same moment. "I will slide my right hand along your arm, and grasp you near the elbow. It will relieve the pressure about your wrist; besides be more convincing to you that there is no trickery."

So saying, he quickly slid the apparatus along her arm, and left it in the position spoken of. This produces a perfect illusion, the clasp with its trick thumb and fingers working to perfection.

This apparatus may also be used in the following manner: Roll up your sleeves and exhibit your hands to the sitter. Tell him you are going to stand behind him and grasp his arms firmly near the shoulders. Take your position immediately under the gas jet. Ask him to please lower the light. Produce the trick clasps, distend them by means of your thumbs and fingers, and after the gas is lowered, grasp the sitter in the manner described. Remove your fingers and thumbs lightly from the clasps and perform various mediumistic evolutions, such as writing a message on a pad or slate placed on the sitter's head; strike him gently on his cheek with a damp glove, etc. When the séance is over, insert your fingers and thumbs in the soldered rings, remove the clasps and conceal them quickly.

EUSAPIA PALADINO.

The materializing medium who has caused the greatest sensation since Home's death is Eusapia

Paladino, an Italian peasant woman. Signor Da-
miani, of Florence, Italy, discovered her alleged psychical powers in 1875, and brought her into notice.
An Italian Count was so impressed with the manifestations witnessed in the presence of the illiterate peas-

FIG. 27.   EUSAPIA PALADINO.

ant woman, that he insisted upon "a commission of
scientific men being called to investigate them." In
the year 1884, this commission held séances with Eusapia, and afterwards declared that the phenomena

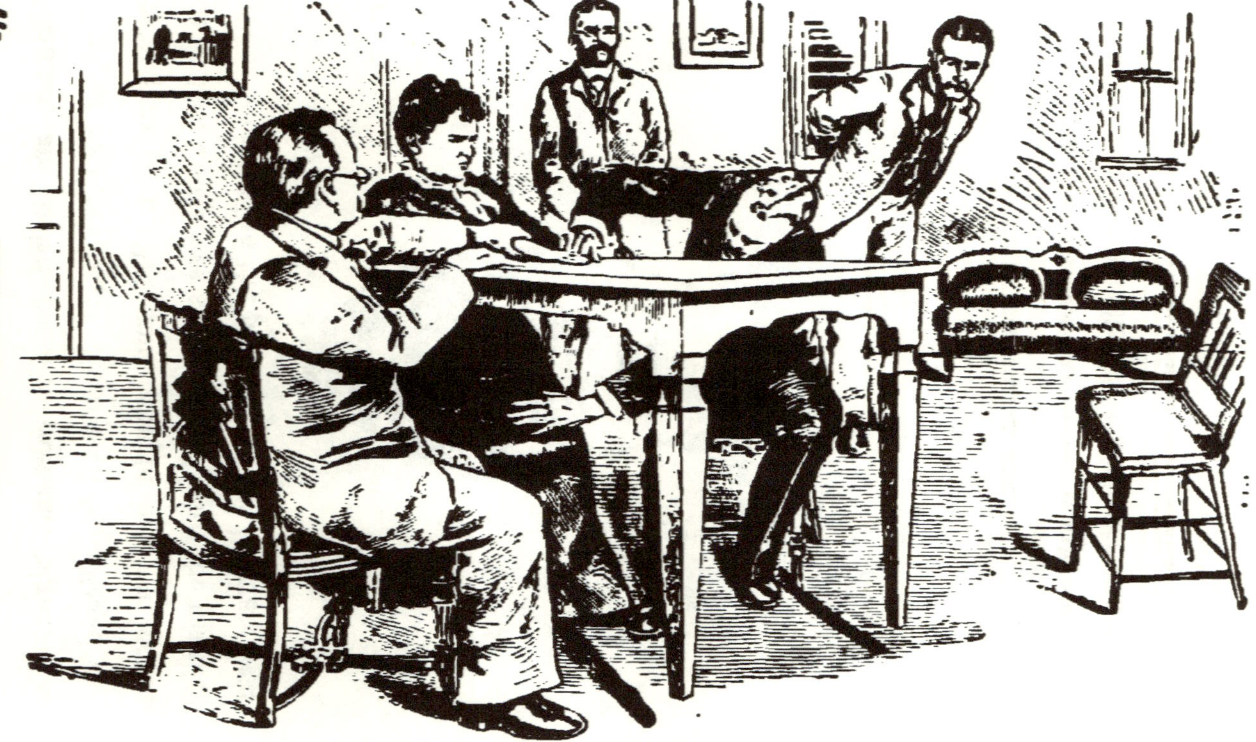

FIG. 25. EUSAPIA BEFORE THE SCIENTISTS.

witnessed were inexplicable, and unquestionably the result of forces transcending ordinary experience. In the year 1892 another commission was formed in Milan to test Eusapia's powers as a medium, and from this period her fame dates, as the most remarkable psychic of modern times. The report drawn up by this commission was signed by Giovanni Schiaparelli, director of the Astronomical Observatory, Milan; Carl du Prel, doctor of philosophy, Munich; Angelo Brofferio, professor of physics in the Royal School of Agriculture, Portici; G. B. Ermacora, doctor of physics; Giorgio Finzi, doctor of physics. At some of the sittings were present Charles Richet and the famous Cesare Lombroso. The conclusion arrived at by these gentlemen was that Eusapia's mediumistic phenomena were most worthy of scientific attention, and were unfathomable. The medium reaped the benefit of this notoriety, and gave sittings to hundreds of investigators among the Italian nobility, charging as high as $500 for a single séance. At last she was exposed by a clever American, Dr. Richard Hodgson, of Boston, secretary of the American branch of the Society for Psychical Research. His account of the affair, communicated to the *New York Herald*, Jan. 10, 1897, is very interesting. Speaking of the report of the Milan commission, he says:

"Their report confessed to seeing and hearing many strange things, although they believed they had the hands and feet of the psychic so closely held that she could have had nothing to do with the manifestations.

"Chairs were moved, bells were rung, imprints of fingers were made on smoked paper and soft clay, apparitions of hands appeared on slightly luminous backgrounds, the chair of the medium and the medium herself were lifted to the table, the sound of trumpets, the contact of a seemingly human face, the touch of human hands, warm and moist, all were felt

"Most of these phenomena were repeated, and the members of the commission were, with two exceptions, satisfied that no known power could have produced them. Professor Richet did not sign the report, but induced Signora Eusapia to go to an island he owned in the Mediterranean, where other exacting tests were made under other scientific eyes. The investigators all agreed that the demonstrations could not be accounted for by ordinary forces.

"I have found in my experience that learned scientific men are the most easily duped of any in the world.   Instead of having a cold, inert piece of matter to investigate by exact processes and microscopic inspections, they had a clever, bright woman doing her best to mystify them.   They could not cope with her.

"Professor Richet replied to an article I wrote, upholding his position, and brought Signora Eusapia Paladino to Cambridge, England, where I joined the investigating committee.   In the party were Professor Lodge, of Liverpool; Professor F. M. C. Meyer, secretary of the British Society for Psychical Research; Professor Richet and Mr. Henry Sedgwick, president of the society.

"I found that the psychic, though giving a great variety of events, confined them to a very limited scope.   She was seated during the tests at the end of a rectangular table and when the table was lifted it rose up directly at the other end.   It was always so arranged that she was in the dark, even if the rest of the table was in the light; in the so-called light séances it was not light, the lamp being placed in an adjoining room.   There were touches, punches and blows given, minor objects moved, some near and some further away; the outline of faces and hands appeared, etc.

"When I came to hold her hands I found a key to the mystery.

"It was chiefly that she made one hand and one foot do the work of both, by adroit substitution. Given a free hand and a free foot, and nearly all the phenomena can be explained. She has very strong, supple hands, with deft fingers and great coolness and intelligence.

"This is the way she substituted one hand for both. She placed one of her hands over A's hand and the other under B's hand. Then, in the movements of the arms during the manifestation, she worked her hands toward each other until they rested one upon the other, with A's hand at the bottom of the pile, B's at the top and both her own, one upon the other, between. To draw out one hand and leave one and yet have the investigators feel that they still had a hand was easy.

"With this hand free and in darkness there were great possibilities. There were strings, also, as I believe, which were attached to different objects and moved them. The dim outlines of faces and hands seen were clever representations of the medium's own free hand in various shapes.

"It is thought that if a medium was kept clapping her hands she could do nothing with them, but one of the investigators found the Signora slapping her face with one hand, producing just the same sound as if her hands met, while the other hand was free to produce mysterious phenomena.

"I have tried the experiment of shifting hands when those who held them knew they were going to be tricked, and yet they did not discover when I made the exchange. I am thoroughly satisfied that Signora Eusapia Paladino is a clever trickster."

Eusapia Paladino was by no means disconcerted by Dr. Hodgson's exposé, but continued giving her séances. At the present writing she is continuing them in France with a number of new illusions. Many who have had sittings with her declare that she is able to move heavy objects without contact. Possibly this is due to jugglery, or it may be due to some psychic force as yet not understood.

F. W. TABOR.

Mr. F. W. Tabor is a materializing medium whose

specialty is the trumpet test for the production of spirit voices. I had a sitting with him at the house of Mr. X, of Washington, D. C., on the night of Jan. 10, 1897. Seven persons, including the medium, sat around an ordinary-sized table in Mr. X—'s drawing room, and formed a chain of hands, in the following manner: Each person placed his or her hands on the table with the thumbs crossed, and the little fingers of each hand touching the little fingers of the sitters on the right and left. A musical box was set going and the light was turned out by Mr. X—, who broke the circle for that purpose, but immediately resumed his old position at the table. A large speaking trumpet of tin about three feet long had been placed upright in the center of the table, and near it was a pad of paper, and pencils. We waited patiently for some little time, the monotony being relieved by operatic airs from the music box, and the singing of hymns by the sitters. There were convulsive twitchings of the hands and feet of the medium, who complained of tingling sensations in those members. The first "phenomena" produced were balls of light dancing like will-o'-the-wisps over the table, and the materialization of a luminous spirit hand. Taps upon the table signalled the arrival of Mr. Tabor's spirit control, "Jim," a little newsboy, of San Francisco, who was run over some years ago by a street car. The medium was the first person who picked up the wounded waif and endeavored to administer to him, but without avail. "Jim" died soon after, and his disembodied spirit became the medium's control. Soon the trumpet arose from the table and floated over the heads of the sitters, and the voice of "Jim" was heard, sepulchral and awe-inspiring, through the instrument. Subsequently, messages of an impersonal character were communicated to Mr. X— and his wife. At one time the trumpet was heard knocking against the chandelier. During the s ance several of the ladies experienced the clasp of a ghostly hand about their wrists, and considerable excitement was occasioned thereby.

It is not a difficult matter to explain this trumpet test. It hinges on one fact, *freedom of the medium's right hand!* In all of these holding tests, the medium employs a subterfuge to release his hands without the knowledge of the sitter on his right. During his convulsive twitchings, he quickly jerks his right hand away, but immediately extends the fingers of his left hand, and connects the index fingers with the little finger of the sitter's left hand, thereby completing the chain, or "battery," as it is technically called. Were the medium to use his thumb in making the connection the secret would be revealed, but the index finger of his left hand sufficiently simulates a little finger, and in the darkness the sitter is deceived. The right hand once released, the medium manipulates the trumpet and the phosphorescent spirit hands to his heart's content. Sometimes he utilizes the telescopic rod, or a pair of steel "crazy tongs," to elevate the trumpet to the ceiling. This holding test is absurdly simple and perhaps for that reason is so convincing.

Mr. Tabor has another method of holding which is far more deceptive than the above. I am indebted to the "Revelations of a Spirit Medium" for an explanation of this test. "The investigators are seated in a circle around the table, male and female alternating. The person sitting on the medium's right—for he sits in the circle—grasps the medium's right wrist in his left hand, while his own right wrist is held by the sitter on his right and this is repeated clear around the circle. This makes each sitter hold the right wrist of his left hand neighbor in his left hand, while his own right hand wrist is held in the left hand of his neighbor on the left. Each one's hands are thus secured and engaged, including the medium's. It will be seen that no one of the sitters can have the use of his or her hands without one or the other of their neighbors knowing it. As each hand was held by a separate person, you cannot understand how he [the medium] could get the use of either of them except the one on his right was a confederate. Such was not the case, and still he *did* have the use of one hand, the right one. But how? He took his place before the light was turned down, and those holding him say he did not let go for an instant during the séance. He did though, after the light was turned out for the purpose of getting his handkerchief to blow his nose. After blowing his nose he requested the sitter to again take his wrist, which is done, but this time it is the wrist of the left hand instead of the right. He has crossed his legs and there is but one knee to be felt, hence the sitter on the right does not feel that she is reaching across the right knee and thinks it is the left knee which she does feel to be the right. He has let his hand slip down until instead of holding the sitter on his left by the wrist he has him by the fingers, thus allowing him a little more distance, and preventing the left hand sitter using the hand to feel about and discover the right hand sitter's hand on the wrist of the hand holding his. You will see, now, that although both sitters are holding the same hand each one thinks he is holding the one on his or her side of the medium. The balance of the séance is easy."

An amusing incident happened during my sitting with Mr. Tabor. Growing somewhat weary waiting for him to "manifest," I determined to undertake some materializations on my own account. I adopted the subterfuge of getting my right hand loose from the lady on my right, and produced the spirit hand that clasped the wrist of several of the sitters in the circle. Mr. X— asked "Jim" if everything was all right in the circle, every hand promptly joined, and the magnetic conditions perfect. "Jim" responded with three affirmative taps on the table top. I congratulate myself on having deceived "Jim," a spirit operating in the fourth dimension of space, and supposedly cognizant of all that was transpiring at the seance. Once, when the medium was floating the trumpet over my head, I grasped the instrument and dashed it on the table. He made no further attempt to manipulate the trumpet in my direction, and very shortly brought the séance to a close. No written communications were received during the evening.

4. Spirit Photography.

You may deceive the human eye, say the advocates of spirit materializations, but you cannot deceive the eye of science, the *photographic camera*. Then they triumphantly produce the spirit photograph as indubitable evidence of the reality of ghostly materializations. "Spirit photography," says the late Alexandre Herrmann, in an article on magic, published in the *Cosmopolitan Magazine*, "was the invention of a man in London, and for ten years Spiritualists accepted the pictures as genuine representations of originals in the spirit land. The snap kodak has superseded the necessity of the explanation of spirit photography."

To be more explicit, there are two ways of producing spirit photographs, by *double printing* and by *double exposure*. In the first, the scene is printed from one negative, and the spirit printed in from another. In the second method, the group with the friendly spook in proper position is arranged, and the lens of the camera uncovered, half of the required exposure being given; then the lens is capped, and the person doing duty as the sheeted ghost gets out of sight, and the exposure is completed. The result is very effective when the picture is printed, the real persons being represented sharp and well defined, while the ghost is but a hazy outline, transparent, through which the background shows.

Every one interested in psychic phenomena who makes a pilgrimage to the Capital of the Nation visits the house of Dr. Theodore Hansmann. For ten years Dr. Hansmann has been an ardent student of Spiritualism, and has had sittings with many celebrated mediums. The walls of his office are literally covered with spirit pictures of famous people of history, executed by spirits under supposed test conditions. There are drawings in color by Raphael, Michel Angelo, and others. In one corner of the room is a book-case filled with slates, upon the surfaces of which are messages from the famous dead, attested by their signatures.

In the fall of 1895, a correspondent of the *New York Herald* interviewed Doctor Hansmann on the subject of spirit photographs, and subsequently visited the United States Bureau of Ethnology, where an interview was had with Mr. Dinwiddie, an expert photographer. Here is the substance of this scond interview, published in the *Herald*, Nov. 9, 1895.

"Dr. Hansmann's collection of 'spirit' photographs is most interesting. There is one with the face of the Empress Josephine, and on the same plate is the head of Professor Darius Lyman, for a long time Chief of the Bureau of Navigation. The head of the Empress Josephine has a diadem around it, and the lights and shadows remind one of the well known portrait of her. On another plate are Grant and Lincoln. Among his other photographs Dr. Hansmann brought out one of a man who was described to me as an Indian agent. Around his head were eleven smaller 'spirit' heads of Indians. In looking at the blue print closely it seemed to me as if I had seen those identical heads— the same as to light, shade and posing—somewhere before.

"I was aided at the Bureau of Ethnology of the Smithsonian Institution by Mr. F. Webb Hodge, the acting director, who on looking at the blue print named the Indians directly; several of the pictures were of Indians still alive. This, of course, imme-

SPIRIT PHOTOGRAPH.
[Taken by the Author.]

diately disposed of the idea of the blue print Indians being spirits.

"Moreover, Mr. Dinwiddie produced the negatives containing the identical portraits of these Indians and made me several proofs, which on a comparison, feature by feature, light for light, and shade for shade, show unquestionably that the faces on the blue print are copies of the portraits made by the photographer of the Bureau of Ethnology.

"Mr. Dinwiddie asked me to sit down for awhile, and offered to make me some spirit photographs. This he did, and the results obtained may be considered as far better examples of the art of 'spirit' photography than those of the medium, Keeler.

"The matter was very simply done. Mr. Dinwiddie asked one of the ladies from the office to come in, and, she consented to pose as a spirit. She was placed before the camera at a distance of about six feet, a red background was given her, so that it might photograph dark, and she was asked to put on a saintly expression. This she did, and Mr. Dinwiddie gave the plate a half-second exposure. Another head was taken on the other side of the plate in much the same manner. After this was done the other or central photograph was taken with an exposure of four seconds, the plate being rather sensitive.

"The plate was then taken to the dark room and developed. The negative came out very well at first, and the halo was put on afterward, when the plate had been dried. The halo was made by rubbing vignetting paste on the back, thus shutting out the light and leaving the paper its original hue. The white shadowy heads which are frequently shown in black coats, and which the mediums claim cannot be explained, are also done in this manner with vignetting paste, the picture being afterward centred over these places, which will be white, the final result showing soft and indefinite, and giving the required spiritual look.

"Mr. Dinwiddie did not attempt to produce the hazy effect, but this is very easily accomplished in the photograph by taking the spirit heads a trifle out of focus. He claims that all of these apparent spiritual manifestations are but tricks of photography, and ones which might be accomplished by the veriest tyro, if he were to study the matter, and give his time to the experiment. It is only a wonder that the mediums do not do more of it.

"The photograph mediums have always claimed

FIG. 30 — SPIRIT PHOTOGRAPH BY PRETENDED MEDIUM

that they were set upon by photographers for business reasons, but Mr. Dinwiddie is employed by the government and has no interests whatever in such a dispute."

The eminent authority on photography, Mr. Walter E. Woodbury, gives many interesting exposes of mediumistic photographs in his work, "Photographic Amusements," which the student of the subject would do well to consult. Fig. 30, taken from "Photographic Amusements" is a reproduction of a "spirit" photograph made by a photographer claiming to be a medium. Says Mr. Woodbury: "Fortunately, however, we were in this case able to expose the fraud. Mr. W. M. Murray, a prominent member of the Society of Amateur Photographers of New York, called our attention to the similarity between one of the 'spirit' images and a portrait painting by Sichel, the artist. A reproduction of the picture (Fig 31) is given herewith, and it will be seen at once that the 'spirit' image is copied from it."

5. Thought Photography.

During the year 1896 considerable stir was created by the investigation of Dr. Hippolyte Baraduc, of Paris, in the line of "Thought Photography," which is of interest to psychic investigators generally. Dr. Baraduc claimed to have gotten photographic impressions of his thoughts, "made without sunlight or electricity or contact of any material kind." These impressions he declared to be subjective, being his own personal vibrations, the result of a force emanating from the human personality, supra-mechanical, or spiritual. The experiments were carried on in a dark room, and according to his statement were highly successful. In a communication to an American correspondent, printed in the *New York Herald*, January 3, 1897, he writes: "I have discovered a human, invisible light, differing altogether from the cathode rays discovered by Prof. Roentgen." Dr. Baraduc advanced the theory that our souls must be considered as centers of luminous forces, owing their existence partly to the attraction and partly to the repulsion of special and potent forces bred of the invisible cosmos."

A number of French scientific journals took up the matter, and discussed "Thought Photography" at length, publishing numerous reproductions of the physician's photographs; but the more conservative journals of England, Germany and America remained silent on the subject, as it seemed to be on the border-

FIG. 31 — SICHEL'S ORIGINAL PICTURE OF FIG. 30.

land between science and charlatanry. On January 11, 1897, the American newspapers contained an item to the effect that Drs. S. Millington Miller and Carleton Simon, of New York City, the former a specialist in brain physiology, and the latter an expert hypnotist, had succeeded in obtaining successful thought photographs on dry plates from two hypnotized subjects. When the subjects were not hypnotized, the physicians reported no results.

As "Thought Photography" is without the pale of known physical laws, stronger evidence is needed to support the claims made for it than that which has been adduced by the French and American investigators. "Thought Photography" once established as a scientific fact, we shall have, perhaps, an explanation of genuine spirit photographs, if such there be.

6. Apparitions of the Dead.

In my chapter on subjective phenomena, I have not recorded any cases of phantasms of the dead, though several interesting examples of such have come under my notice. I have thought it better to refer the reader to the voluminous reports of the Society for Psychical Research (England). In regard to these cases, the Society has reached the following conclusion: *Between deaths and apparitions of dying persons a connection exists which is not due to chance alone. This we hold as a proved fact.*

The "*Literary Digest*," January 12, 1895, in reviewing this report, says: "Inquiries were instituted in 17,000 cases of alleged apparitions. These inquiries elicited 1,249 replies from persons [in England and Wales] who affirmed that they themselves had seen the apparitions. Then the Society by further inquiries and cross-examinations sifted out all but eighty of these as discredited in some way, by error of memory or illusions of identity, or for some other reason, or which could be accounted for by common psychical laws. Of these eighty, fifty more were thrown out, to be on the safe side, and the remaining thirty are used as a basis for scientific consideration. All these consisted of apparitions of dead persons appearing to others within twelve hours after death, and many of them appearing at the very hour and even the very minute of death. The full account of the investigation is published in the tenth volume of the Society's Reports, under the title, 'A Census of Hallucinations,' and Prof. J. H. Hyslop, of Columbia College, wrote an article giving the gist of the report and his comments in the '*Independent*,' (December 27, 1895), from which I cull these few notable paragraphs:

" 'The committee which conducted the research reasons as follows: Since the death rate of England is 19.15 out of every thousand, the chances of any person's dying on any particular day are one in 19,000 (the ratio of 19.15 to 365 times 1,000). Out of 19,000 death apparitions, therefore, one can be explained as à simple coincidence. But thirty apparitions out of 1,300 cases is in the proportion of 440 out of 19,000, so that to refer these thirty well-authenticated apparitions to coincidence is deemed impossible.'

"And further on:

" 'This is remarkable language for the signatures of Prof. and Mrs. Sidgwick, than whom few harder-headed skeptics could be found. It is more than borne out, however, by a consideration which the committee does not mention, but which the facts entirely justify, and it is that since many of the apparitions occurred not merely on the day, but at the very hour or minute of death, the improbability of their explanation by chance is really much greater than the figures here given. That the apparition should occur within the hour of death the chance should be 1 to 356,000, or at the minute of death 1 to 21,360,000. To get 30 cases, therefore, brought down to these limits we should have to collect thirty times these numbers of apparitions. Either these statistics are of no value in a study of this kind, or the Society's claim is made out that there is either a telepathic communication between the dying and those who see their apparitions, or some causal connection not yet defined or determined by science. That this connection may be due to favorable conditions in the subject of the hallucination is admitted by the committee, if the person having the apparition is suffering from grief or anxiety about the person concerned. But it has two replies to such a criticism. The first is the query how and why under the circumstances does this effect coincide generally with the death of the person concerned, when anxiety is extended over a considerable period. The second is a still more triumphant reply, and it is that a large number of the cases show that the subject of the apparition has no knowledge of the dying person's sickness, place, or condition. In that case there is no alternative to searching elsewhere for the cause. If telepathy or thought transference will not explain the connection, resort must be had to some most extraordinary hypothesis. Most persons will probably accept telepathy as the easiest way out of the difficulty, though I am not sure that we are limited to this, the easiest explanation.'

"Professor Hyslop then proceeds to consider the effect of the committee's conclusion upon existing theories and speculations regarding the relations between mind and matter, and foresees with gratification as well as apprehension the revolt likely to be initiated against materialism and which may go so far as to discredit science and carry us far back to the credulous conditions of the Middle Ages. He says:

" 'The point which the investigations of the Society for Psychical Research have already reached creates a question of transcendent interest, no matter what the solution of it may be, and will stimulate in the near future an amount of psychological and theological speculation of the most hasty and crude sort, which it will require the profoundest knowledge of mental phenomena, normal and abnormal, and the best methods of science to counteract, and to keep within the limits of sober reason. The hardly won conquests of intellectual freedom and self-control can easily be overthrown by a reaction that will know no bounds and which it will be impossible to regulate. Though there may be some moral gain from the change of beliefs, as will no doubt be the case in the long run, we have too recently escaped the intellectual, religious, and political tyranny of the Middle Ages to contemplate the immediate consequences of the reaction with any complacency. But no one can calculate the enormous effect upon intellectual, social, and political conditions which would ensure upon the reconciliation of science and religion by the proof of immortality."

IV. CONCLUSIONS.

In my investigations of the physical phenomena of modern spiritualism, I have come to the following conclusion: While the majority of mediumistic manifestations are due to conjuring, there is a class of cases not ascribable to trickery, namely, those coming within the domain of psychic force—as exemplified by the experiments of Gasparin, Crookes, Lodge, Asakoff and Coues. In regard to the subjective phenomena, I am convinced that the recently annunciated law of telepathy will account for them. *I discredit the theory of spirit intervention.* If this be a correct conclusion, is there anything in mediumistic phenomena that will contribute to the solution of the problem of the immortality of the soul? I think there is. The existence of a subjective or subliminal consciousness in man, as illustrated in the phenomena mentioned, seems to indicate that the human personality is really a spiritual entity, possessed of unknown resources, and capable of preserving its identity despite the shock of time and the grave. Hudson says: "It is clear that the power of telepathy has nothing in common with objective methods of communications between mind and mind; and that it is not the product of muscle or nerve or any physiological combination whatever, but rather sets these at naught, with their implications of space and time. . . . When disease seizes the physical frame and the body grows feeble, the objective mind invariably grows correspondingly weak. . . . In the meantime, as the objective mind ceases to perform its functions, the subjective mind is most active and powerful. The individual may never before have exhibited any psychic power, and may never have consciously produced any psychic phenomena; yet at the supreme moment his soul is in active communication with loved ones at a distance, and the death message is often, when psychic conditions are favorable, consciously received. The records of telepathy demonstrate this proposition. Nay, more; they may be cited to show that in the hour of death the soul is capable of projecting a phantasm of such strength and objectivity that it may be an object of personal experience to those for whom it is intended. Moreover, it has happened that telepathic messages have been sent by the dying, at the moment of dissolution, giving all the particulars of the tragedy, when the death was caused by an unexpected blow which crushed the skull of the victim. It is obvious that in such cases it is impossible that the objective mind could have participated in the transaction. The evidence is indeed overwhelming, that, no matter what form death may assume, whether caused by lingering disease, old age, or violence, the subjective mind is never weakened by its approach or its presence. On the other hand, that the objective mind weakens with the body and perishes with the brain, is a fact confirmed by every-day observation and universal experience."

This hypothesis of the objective and subjective minds has been criticised by many psychologists on the ground of its extreme dualism. No such dualism exists, they contend. However, Hudson's theory is only a working hypothesis at best, to explain certain extraordinary facts in human experience. Future investigators may be able to throw more light on the subject. But this one thing may be enunciated: *Telepathy is an incontrovertible fact*, account for it as you may, a physical force or a spiritual energy. If physical, then it does not follow any of the known operations of physical laws as established by modern science, especially in the case of transmission of thought at a distance.

It is true, that all evidence in support of telepathic communications is more or less *ex parte* in character, and does not possess that validity which orthodox science requires of investigators. Any student of the physical laws of matter can make investigations for himself, and at any time, provided he has the proper apparatus. Explain to a person that water is composed of two gases, oxygen and hydrogen, and he can easily verify the fact for himself by combining the gases, in the combination of H_2O, and afterwards liberate them by a current of electricity. But experiments in telepathy and clairvoyance cannot be made at will; they are isolated in character, and consequently are regarded with suspicion by orthodox science. Besides this, they transcend the materialistic theories of science as regards the universe, and one is almost compelled to use the old metaphysical terms of mind and matter, body and soul, in describing the phenomena.

It is an undoubted fact that science has broken away from the old theory regarding the distinction between mind and matter. Says Prof. Wm. Romaine Newbold,

"In the scientific world it has fallen into such disfavor that in many circles it is almost as disgraceful to avow belief in it as in witchcraft or ghosts." We have todaya school of "physiological-psychology," calling itself "psychology without a soul." This school is devoted to the laboratory method of studying mind. "The laboratory method," says Roark, in his "Psychology in Education," "is concerned mostly with *physiological* psychology, which is, after all, only *physiology*, even though it be the physiology of the nervous system and the special organs of sense—the material tools of the mind. And after physiological psychology has had its rather prolix say, causal connection of the physical organs with psychic action is as obscure and impossible of explanation as ever. But the laboratory method can be of excellent service in determining the material conditions of mental action, in detecting special deficiencies and weaknesses, and in accumulating valuable statistics along these lines.

"It has been asserted that no science can claim to be exact until it can be reduced to formulas of weights and measures. The assertion begs the question for the materialists. We shall probably never be able to weigh an idea or measure the cubic contents of the memory; but the rapidity with which ideas are formed or reproduced by memory has been measured in many particular instances, and the circumstances that retard or accelerate their formation or reproduction have been positively ascertained and classified."

That it is possible to explain all mental phenomena in terms of physics is by no means the unanimous verdict of scientific men. A small group of students of late years have detached themselves from the purely materialistic school and broken ground in the region of the supernormal Says Professor Newbold (*Popular Science Monthly*, January, 1897): "In the supernormal field, the facts already reported, should they be substantiated by further inquiry, would go far towards showing that consciousness is an entity governed by laws and possessed of powers incapable of expression in material conceptions.

"I do not myself regard the theory of independence [of mind and body] as proved, but I think we have enough evidence for it to destroy in any candid mind that considers it that absolute credulity as to its possibility which at present characterizes the average man of science."

PART SECOND.

MADAME BLAVATSKY AND THE THEO-SOPHISTS.

1. The Priestess.

The greatest "fantaisiste" of modern tim:s was Madame Blavatsky, spirit medium, Priestess of Isis, and founder of the Theosophical Society. Her life is one long catalogue of wonders. In appearance she was enormously fat, had a harsh, disagreeable voice, and a violent temper, dressed in a slovenly manner, usually in loose wrappers, smoked cigarettes incessantly, and cared little or nothing for the conventionalities of life. But in spite of all—unprepossessing appearance and gross habits—she exercised a powerful personal magnetism over those who came in contact with her. She was the Sphinx of the second half of this Century; a Pythoness in tinsel robes who strutted across the world's stage "full of sound and fury," and disappeared from view behind the dark veil of Isis, which she, the fin-de-siecle prophetess, tried to draw aside during her earthly career.

In searching for facts concerning the life of this really remarkable woman—remarkable for the influence she has exerted upon the thought of this latter end of the nineteenth century—I have read all that has been written about her by prominent Theosophists, have talked with many who knew her intimately, and now endeavor to present the truth concerning her and her career. The leading work on the subject is "Incidents in the Life of Madame Blavatsky," compiled from information supplied by her relatives and friends, and edited by A. P. Sinnett, author of "The Occult World." The frontispiece to the book is a reproduction of a portrait of Madame Blavatsky, painted by H. Schmiechen, and represents the lady seated on the steps of an ancient ruin, holding a parchment in her hand. She is garbed somewhat after the fashion of a Cumacan Sibyl and gazes straight before her with the deep unfathomable eyes of a mystic, as if she were reading the profound riddles of the ages, and beholding the sands of Time falling hot and swift into the glass of eternity—

"And all things creeping to a day of doom."

FIG. 32 — MADAME BLAVATSKY

Sinnett's life of the High Priestess is a strange con-
coction of monstrous absurdities; it is full of the weird-
est happenings that were ever vouchsafed to mortal.
We cannot put much faith in this biography, and must
delve in other mines for information; but some of the
remarkable passages of the book are worth perusing,
particularly if the reader be prone to midnight. musings of a ghostly character.

Helena Petrovna Blavatsky, the daughter of Col.
Peter Hahn of the Russian Army, and granddaughter
of General Alexis Hahn von Rottenstern Hahn (a
noble family of Mecklenburg, Germany, settled
in Russia), was born in Eskaterinoslaw, in the
south of Russia, in 1831. "She had," says Sinnett,
"a strange childhood, replete with abnormal oc-
currences. The year of her birth was fatal
for Russia, as for all Europe, owing to the first visit
of the cholera, that terrible plague that decimated
from 1830 to 1832 in turn nearly every town of the
Continent. . . . . Her birth was quickened by
several deaths in the house, and she was ushered into
the world amid coffins and desolation, on the night between July 30th and 31st, weak and apparently no den-
izen of this world." A hurried baptism was given lest

the child die in original sin, and the ceremony was that of the Greek Church. During the orthodox baptismal rite no person is allowed to sit, but a child aunt of the baby, tired of standing for nearly an hour, settled down upon the floor, just behind the officiating priest. No one perceived her, as she sat nodding drowsily. The ceremony was nearing its close. The sponsors were just in the act of renouncing the Evil One and his deeds, a renunciation emphasized in the Greek Church by thrice spitting upon the invisible enemy, when the little lady, toying with her lighted taper at the feet of the crowd, inadvertantly set fire to the long flowing robes of the priest, no one remarking the accident till it was too late. The result was an immediate conflagration, during which several persons—chiefly the old priest—were severely burnt That was another bad omen, according to the superstitious beliefs of orthodox Russia: and the innocent cause of it, the future Madame Blavatsky, was doomed from that day, in the eyes of all the town, to an eve itful, troubled life.

"Mlle. Hahn was born, of course, with all the characteristics of what is known in Spiritualism as mediumship in the most extraordinary degree, also with gifts as a clairvoyant of an almost equally unexampled order. On various occasions while apparently in an ordinary sleep, she would answer questions, put by persons who took hold of her hand, about lost property, etc., as though she were a sibyl entranced. For years she would, in childish impulse, shock strangers with whom she came in contact, and visitors to the house, by looking them intently in the face and telling them they would die at such and such a time, or she would prophesy to them some accident or misfortune that would befall them. And since her prognostications usually came true, she was the terror, in this respect, of the domestic circle."

Madame V. P. Jelihowsy, a sister of the seeress, has furnished to the world many extraordinary stories of Mme. Blavatsky's childhood, published in various Russian periodicals. At the age of eleven the Sibyl lost her mother, and went to live with her grandparents at Saratow, her grandfather being civil governor of the place. The family mansion was a lumbering old country place "full of subterraneous galleries, long abandoned passages, turrets, and most weird nooks and corners. It looked more like a mediaeval ruined castle than a building of the last century." The ghosts of

martyred serfs were supposed to haunt the uncanny
building, and strange legends were told by the old
family servants of weir-wolves and goblins that
prowled about the dark forests of the estate. Here, in
this House of Usher, the Sibyl lived and dreamed, and
at this period exhibited many abnormal psychic pe-
culiarities, ascribed by her orthodox governess and
nurses of the Greek Church to possession by the devil.
She had at times ungovernable fits of temper; she
would ride any Cossack horse on the place astride a
man's saddle; go into trances and scare everyone from
the master of the mansion down to the humblest
vodka drinker on the estate.

In 1848, at the age of 17, she married General
Count Blavatsky, a gouty old Russian of 70, whom
she called "the plumed raven," but left him after
a brief period of marital infelicity. From this
time dates her career as a thaumaturgist. She
travelled through India and made an honest attempt
to penetrate into the mysterious confines of Thibet,
but succeeded in getting only a few miles from the
frontier, owing to the fanaticism of the natives.

In India, as elsewhere, she was accused of being a
Russian spy and was generally regarded with suspi-

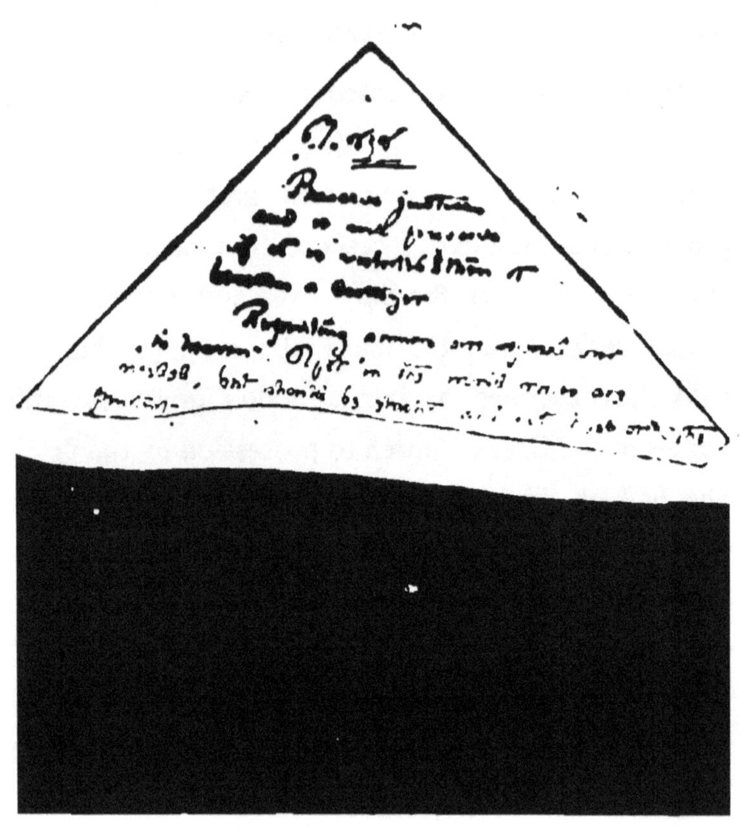

FIG. 33 — MAHATMA LETTER.

cion by the police authorities. After some months of erratic wanderings she reappeared in Russia, this time in Tiflis, at the residence of a relative, Prince ——. It was a gloomy, grewsome chateau, well suited for Spiritualistic séances, and Madame Blavatsky, it is claimed, frightened the guests during the long winter evenings with table-tippings, spirit rappings, etc. It was then the tall candles in the drawing-room burnt low, the gobelin tapestry rustled, sighs were heard, strange music "resounded in the air," and luminous forms were seen trailing their ghostly garments across the "tufted floor."

The gossipy Madame de Jelihowsy, in her reminiscences, classifies the phenomena, witnessed in the presence of her Sibylline sister, as follows:

1. Direct and perfectly clearly written and verbal answers to mental questions—or "thought reading."

2. Private secrets, unknown to all but the interested party, divulged, [especially in the case of those persons who mentioned insulting doubts].

3. Change of weight in furniture and persons at will.

4. Letters from unknown correspondents, and immediate answers written to queries made, and found in the most out-of-the-way mysterious places.

5. Appearance of objects unclaimed by anyone present.

6. Sounds of musical notes in the air wherever Madame Blavatsky desired they should resound.

In the year 1858, the High Priestess was at the house of General Yakontoff at Pskoff, Russia. One night when the drawing-room was full of visitors, she began to describe the mediumistic feat of making light objects heavy and heavy objects light.

"Can you perform such a miracle?" ironically asked her brother, Leonide de Hahn, who always doubted his sister's occult powers.

"I can," was the firm reply.

De Hahn went to a small chess table, lifted it as though it were a feather, and said: "Suppose you try your powers on this."

"With pleasure!" replied Mme. Blavatsky. "Place the table on the floor, and step aside for a minute." He complied with her request.

She fixed her large blue eyes intently upon the chess table and said without removing her gaze, "Lift it now."

The young man exerted all his strength, but the

table would not budge an inch. Another guest tried with the same result, but the wood only cracked, yielding to no effort.

"Now, lift it," said Madame Blavatsky calmly, whereupon De Hahn picked it up with the greatest ease. Loud applause greeted this extraordinary feat, and the skeptical brother, so say the occultists, was utterly nonplussed.

Madame Blavatsky, as recorded by Sinnett, stated afterwards that the above phenomenon could be produced in two different ways: "First, through the exercise of her own will directing the magnetic currents so that the pressure on the table became such that no physical force could move it; second, through the action of those beings with whom she was in constant communication, and who, although unseen, were able to hold the table against all opposition."

The writer has seen similar feats performed by hypnotizers with good subjects without the intervention of any ghostly intelligences.

In 1870 the Priestess of Isis journeyed through Egypt in company with a certain Countess K—, and endeavored to form a Spiritualistic society at Cairo, for the investigation of psychic phenomena, but things growing unpleasant for her she left the land of pyramids and papyri in hot haste. It is related of her that during this Egyptian sojourn she spent one night in the King's sepulchre in the bowels of the Great Pyramid of Cheops, sleeping in the very sarcophagus where once reposed the mummy of a Pharoah. Weird sights were seen by the entranced occultist and strange sounds were heard on that eventful occasion within the shadowy mortuary chamber of the pyramid. At times she would let fall mysterious hints of what she saw that night, but they were as incomprehensible as the riddles of the fabled Sphinx.

Countess Paschkoff chronicles a curious story about the Priestess of Isis, which reminds one somewhat of the last chapter in Bulwer's occult novel, "A Strange Story." The Countess relates that she was once travelling between Baalbec and the river Orontes, and in the desert came across the caravan belonging to Madame Blavatsky. They joined company and towards nightfall pitched camp near the village of El Marsum amid some ancient ruins. Among the relics of a Pagan civilization stood a great monument covered with outlandish hieroglyphics. The Countess was curious to decipher the inscriptions, and begged Madame Blavatsky to unravel their meaning, but the Priestess of Isis, notwithstanding her great archaeological knowledge, was unable to do so. However, she said: "Wait until night, and we shall see!" When the ruins were wrapped in sombre shadow, Mme. Blavatsky drew a great circle upon the ground about the monument, and invited the Countess to stand within the mystic confines. A fire was built and upon it were thrown various aromatic herbs and incense. Cabalistic spells were recited by the sorceress, as the smoke from the incense ascended, and then she thrice commanded the spirit to whom the monument was erected to appear. Soon the cloud of smoke from the burning incense assumed the shape of an old man with a long white beard. A voice from a distance pierced the misty image, and spoke: "I am Hiero, one of the priests of a great temple erected to the gods, that stood upon this spot. This monument was the altar. Behold!" No sooner were the words pronounced than a phantasmagoric vision of a gigantic temple appeared, supported by ponderous columns, and a great city was seen covering the distant plain, but all soon faded into thin air.

This story was related to a select coterie of occultists assembled in social conclave at the headquarters in New York. The question is, had the charming Russian Countess dreamed this, or was she trying to exploit herself as a traveler who had come "out of the mysterious East" and had seen strange things?

We next hear of the famous occultist in the United States, where she associated chiefly with spirit-mediums, enchanters, professional clairvoyants, and the like.

"At this period of her career she had not,"* says Dr. Eliott Coues, a learned investigator of psychic phenomena, "been metamorphosed into a Theosophist. She was simply exploiting as a Spiritualistic medium. Her most familiar spook was a ghostly fiction named 'John King.' This fellow is supposed to have been a pirate, condemned for his atrocities to serve earth-bound for a term of years, and to present himself at materializing séances on call. Any medium who personates this ghost puts on a heavy black horse-hair beard and a white bed sheet and talks in sepulchral chest tones. John is as standard and sure-enough a ghost as ever appeared before the public. Most of the leading mediums, both in Europe and America,

---

* Communication to *New York Sun*, 1890.

keep him in stock. I have often seen the old fellow in New York, Philadelphia, and Washington through more mediums that I can remember the names of. Our late Minister to Portugul, Mr. J. O'Sullivan, has a photograph of him at full length, floating in space, holding up a peculiar globe of light shaped like a glass decanter. This trustworthy likeness was taken in Europe, and I think in Russia, but am not sure on that point. I once had the pleasure of introducing the pirate king to my friend Prof. Alfred Russel Wallace, in the person of Pierre L. O. A. Keeler, a noted medium of Washington.

"But the connection between the pirate and my story is this: Madame Blavatsky was exploiting King at the time of which I speak, and several of her letters to friends, which I have read, are curiously scribbled in red and blue pencil with sentences and signatures of 'John King,' just as, later on, 'Koot Hoomi' used to miraculously precipitate himself upon her stationery in all sorts of colored crayons. And, by the way, I may call the reader's attention to the fact that while the ingenious creature was operating in Cairo, her Mahatmas were of the Egyptian order of architecture, and located in the ruins of Thebes or Karnak. They were not put in turbans and shifted to Thibet till late in 1879."

In 1875, while residing in New York, Madame Blavatsky conceived the idea of establishing a Theosophical Society. Stupendous thought! Cagliostro in the eighteenth century founded his Egyptian Free-Masonry for the re-generation of mankind, and Blavatsky in the nineteenth century laid the corner stone of modern Theosophy for a similar purpose. Cagliostro had his High Priestess in the person of a beautiful wife, Lorenza Feliciani, and Blavatsky her Hierophant in the somewhat prosaic guise of a New York reporter, Col. Olcott, since then a famous personage in occult circles.

During the Civil War, Olcott served in the Quartermaster's Department of the Army and afterwards held a position in the Internal Revenue Service of the United States. In 18— he was a newspaper man in New York, and was sent by the *Graphic* to investigate the alleged Spiritualistic phenomena transpiring in the Eddy family in Chittenden, Vermont. There he met Madame Blavatsky. It was his fate.

Col. Olcott's description of his first sight of Mme. Blavatsky is interesting:

"The dinner at Eddy's was at noon, and it was from the entrance door of the bare and comfortless dining-room that Kappes and I first saw H. P. B. She had arrived shortly before noon with a French Canadian

FIG. 35. COL. H. S. OLCOTT.

lady, and they were at table as we entered. My eye was first attracted by a scarlet Garibaldian shirt the former wore, as being in vivid contrast with the dull colors around. Her hair was then a thick blonde mop, worn shorter than the shoulders, and it stood out from her head, silken, soft, and crinkled to the roots, like the fleece of a Cotswold ewe. This and the red shirt were what struck my attention before I took in the picture of her features. It was a massive Kalmuck face, contrasting in its suggestion of power, culture, and imperiousness, as strangely with the commonplace visages about the room, as her red garment did with the gray and white tones of the wall and woodwork, and the dull costumes of the rest of the guests. All sorts of cranky people were continually coming and going at Eddy's, to see the mediumistic phenomena, and it only struck me on seeing this eccentric lady that this was but one more of the sort. Pausing on the door-sill, I whispered to Kappes, 'Good gracious! look at *that* specimen, will you!' I went straight across and took a seat opposite her to indulge my favorite habit of character-study."

Commenting on this meeting, J. Ransom Bridges, in the *Arena*, for April, 1895, remarks: "After dinner Colonel Olcott scraped an acquaintance by opportunely offering her a light for a cigarette which she proceeded to roll for herself. This 'light' must have been charged with Theosophical *karma*, for the burning match or end of a lighted cigar—the Colonel does not specify—lit a train of causes and their effects which now are making history and are world-wide in

Pledge
of Secrisy
To be read aloud by each member in the
presence of the society
before signing the roll

In accepting Fellowship in the society
organized under the foregoing preamble
and by laws I hereby promise to maintain
absolute secrecy respecting the proceedings of
the said society including its investigations and
experiments except in so far as publication may
be authorized by the society or council, and I
hereby pledge my word of honor for the
strict observance of this covenant

No	Name	Address
1	H. S. Olcott	7 Beekman St.
2	H. P. Blavatsky	433 W. 34th St. N.Y.
3		
4	Henry J. Newton	128 West 43d St. N.Y.
5	Geo. H. Felt	313 W. 59 St.
6	John Storer Cobb	67 & 69 William St.
7	Emma H. Britten	118 West 26 St. N.Y.
8	Wm. Q. Judge	71 Broadway N.Y.
9	Robt. Cummings	742 Lexington Av.
10	Chas E. Whiting	33 Sterling Place Bkn
11	R. B. Westbrook	
12	D. E. de Lara	625 Lexington ave

FIG. 36. OATH OF SECRECY TAKEN BY CHARTER MEMBERS OF THE THEO
SOPHICAL SOCIETY.

[Kindness of the *New York Herald*.]

their importance. So confirmed a pessimist on Theosophical questions as Henry Sidgwick of the London Society for Psychical Research, says, 'Even if it [the Theosophical Society] were to expire next year, its twenty years' existence would be a phenomenon of some interest for a historian of European society in the nineteenth century.' "

The seances at the Eddy house must have been character studies indeed. The place where the ghosts were materialized was a large apartment over the dining room of the ancient homestead. A dark closet, at one end of the room, with a rough blanket stretched across it, served as a cabinet. Red Indians and pirates were the favorite materializations, but when Madame Blavatsky appeared on the scene, ghosts of Turks, Kurdish cavaliers, and Kalmucks visited this earthly scene, much to the surprise of every one. Olcott cites this fact as evidence of the genuineness of the materializations, remarking, "how could the ignorant Eddy boys, rough, rude, uncultured farmers, get the costumes and accessories for characters of this kind in a remote Vermont village."

2. What is Theosophy.

Let us turn aside at this juncture to ask, "What is Theosophy." The word Theosophy (Theosophia—divine knowledge) appears to have been used about the Third century, A. D., by the Neo-Platonists, or Gnostics of Alexandria, but the great principles of the doctrine, however, were taught hundreds of years prior to the mystical school established at Alexandria. "It is not," says an interesting writer on the subject, "an outgrowth of Buddhism although many Buddhists see in its doctrines the reflection of Buddha. It proposes to give its followers the esoteric, or inner-spiritual meaning of the great religious teachers of the world. It asserts repeated re-incarnations, or rebirths of the soul on earth, until it is fully purged of evil, and becomes fit to be absorbed into the Deity whence it came, gaining thereby Nirvana, or unconsciousness." Some Theosophists claim that Nirvana is not a state of unconsciousness, but just the converse, a state of the most intensified consciousness, during which the soul remembers all of its previous incarnations.

Madame Blavatsky claimed that "there exists in Thibet a brotherhood whose members have acquired a power over Nature which enables them to perform wonders beyond the reach of ordinary men. She declared herself to be a *chela*, or disciple of these brothers (spoken of also as 'Adepts' and as 'Mahatmas'), and asserted that they took a special interest in the Theosophical Society and all initiates in occult lore, being able to cause apparitions of themselves in places where their bodies were not; and that they not only appeared but communicated intelligently with those whom they thus visited and themselves perceived what was going on where their phantoms appeared." This phantasmal appearance she called the projection of the *astral* form. Many of the phenomena witnessed in the presence of the Sibyl were supposed to be the work of the mystic brotherhood who took so peculiar an interest in the Theosophical Society and its members. The Madame did not claim to be the founder of a new religious faith, but simply the reviver of a creed that has slumbered in the Orient for centuries, and declared herself to be the Messenger of these Mahatmas to the scoffing Western world.

Speaking of the Mahatmas, she says in "Isis Unveiled": * * * "Travelers have met these adepts on the shores of the sacred Ganges, brushed against them on the silent ruins of Thebes, and in the mysterious deserted chambers of Luxor. Within the halls upon whose blue and golden vaults the weird signs attract attention, but whose secret meaning is never penetrated by the idle gazers, they have been seen, but seldom recognized. Historical memoirs have recorded their presence in the brilliantly illuminated salons of European aristocracy. They have been encountered again on the arid and desolate plains of the Great Sahara, or in the caves of Elephanta. They may be found everywhere, but make themselves known only to those who have devoted their lives to unselfish study, and are not likely to turn back."

The Theosophical Society was organized in New York, Nov. 17, 1875.

Mr. Arthur Lillie, in his interesting work, "Madame Blavatsky and Her Theosophy," speaking about the founding of the Society, says:

"Its moving spirit was a Mr. Felt, who had visited Egypt and studied its antiquities. He was a student also of the Kabbala; and he had a somewhat eccentric theory that the dog-headed and hawk-headed figures painted on the Egyptian monuments were not mere symbols, but accurate portraits of the 'Elementals.' He professed to be able to evoke and control them.

He announced that he had discovered the secret 'for-
mularies' of the old Egyptian magicians. Plainly, the
Theosophical Society at starting was an Egyptian
school of occultism. Indeed Colonel Olcott, who fur-
nishes these details ('Diary Leaves' in the *Theosophist*, November to December, 1892), lets out that the
first title suggested was the 'Egyptological Society.' "

There were strange reports set afloat at the time of
the organization of the Society of the mysterious appearance of a Hindoo adept in his astral body at the
"lamasery" on Forty-seventh street. It was said to
be that of a certain Mahatma Koot Hoomi. Olcott
declared that the adept left behind him as a souvenir
of his presence, a turban, which was exhibited on all
occasions by the enterprising Hierophant. William
Q. Judge, a noted writer on Spiritualism, who had
met the Madame at Irving Place in the winter of 1874,
joined the Society about this time, and became an
earnest advocate of the secret doctrine. One wintry
evening in March, 1889, Mr. Judge attended a meeting of the New York Anthropological Society, and
told the audience all about the spectral gentleman,
Koot Hoomi. He said:

"The parent society (Theosophical) was founded in

America by Madame Blavatsky, who gathered about her a few interested people and began the great work. They held a meeting to frame a constitution (1875), etc., but before anything had been accomplished a strangely foreign Hindoo, dressed in the peculiar garb

FIG. 37. WILLIAM Q. JUDGE.
[Reproduced by courtesy of the *New York Herald.*]

of his country, came before them, and, leaving a package, vanished, and no one knew whither he came or went. On opening the package they found the necessary forms of organization, rules, etc., which were adopted. The inference to be drawn was, that the strange visitor was a Mahatma, interested in the foundation of the Society."

And so Blavatskyism flourished, and the Society gathered in disciples from all quarters. Men without definite creeds are ever willing to embrace anything that savors of the mysterious, however absurd the tenets of the new doctrine may be. The objects of the Theosophical Society, as set forth in a number of *Lucifer*, the organ of the cult, published in July, 1890, are stated to be:

"1. To form a nucleus of a Universal Brotherhood of Humanity without distinction of race, creed, sex, or color.

"2. To promote the study of Aryan and other Eastern literatures, religions and sciences.

"3. To investigate laws of Nature and the psychical powers of man."

There is nothing of cant or humbug about the above articles. A society founded for the prosecution of such researches seems laudable enough. Oriental scholars and scientists have been working in this field for many years. But the investigations, as conducted under the Blavatsky régime, have savored so of char-

latanism that many earnest, truth-seeking Theosophists have withdrawn from the Society.

After seeing the Society well established, Madame
Blavatsky went to India. Her career in that country
was a checkered one. From this period dates the
exposé of the Mahatma miracles. The story reads
like a romance by Marie Corelli. Let us begin at the
beginning. The headquarters of the Society was first
established at Bombay, thence removed to Madras and
afterwards to Adyar. A certain M. and Mme. Coulomb, trusted friends of Madame Blavatsky, were
made librarian and assistant corresponding secretary
respectively of the Society, and took up their residence
in the building known as the headquarters—a ramb-
ling East Indian bungalow, such as figure in Rudyard
Kipling's stories of Oriental life. Marvellous phenomena, of an occult nature, alleged to have taken place
there, were attested by many Theosophists. Mysterious, ghostly appearances of Mahatmas were seen, and
messages were constantly received by supernatural
means. One of the apartments of the bungalow was
denominated the Occult Room, and in this room was
a sort of cupboard against the wall, known as the
Shrine. In this shrine the ghostly missives were re-

ceived and from it were sent. Skeptics were convinced, and occult lodges spread rapidly over India among the dreamy, marvel-loving natives. But affairs were not destined to sail smoothly. There came a rift within the lute—Madame Blavatsky quarreled with her trusted lieutenants, the Coulombs! In May, 1884, M. and Mme. Coulomb were expelled from the Society by the General Council, during the absence of the High Priestess and Col. Olcott in Europe. The Coulombs, who had grown weary of a life of imposture, or were actuated by the more ignoble motive of revenge, made a complete exposé of the secret working of the Inner Brotherhood. They published portions of Madame Blavatsky's correspondence in the *Madras Christian College Magazine*, for September and October, 1884; letters written to the Coulombs, directing them to prepare certain impostures and letters written by the High Priestess, under the signature of Koot Hoomi, the mythical adept.* This correspondence unquestionably implicated the Sibyl in a conspiracy to fraudulently produce occult phenomena. She declared them to be, in whole, or in part, forgeries. At this juncture

---

* NOTE—These letters were purchased from the *Christian College Magazine* by Dr. Elliot Coues, of Washington, D. C.

the London Society for Psychical Research sent Mr. Richard Hodgson, B. A., scholar of St. John's College, Cambridge, England, to India to investigate the entire matter in the interest of science.

He left England November, 1884, and remained in the East till April, 1885. During this period Blavatskyism was sifted to the bottom. Mr. Hodgson's report covers several hundred pages, and proves conclusively that the occult phenomena of Madame Blavatsky and her co-adjutors are unworthy of credence. In his volume he gives diagrams of the trap-doors and machinery of the shrine and the occult room, and facsimiles of Madame Blavatsky's handwriting, which proved to be identical with that of Koot Hoomi, or *Cute* Hoomi, as the critics dubbed him. He shows that the Coulombs had told the plain unvarnished truth so far as their disclosures went; and he stigmatizes the Priestess of Isis in the following language:

"1. She has been engaged in a long continued combination with other persons to produce by ordinary means a series of apparent marvels for the support of the Theosophic movement.

"2. That in particular the shrine at Adyar through which letters purporting to come from Mahatmas were received, was elaborately arranged with a view to the secret insertion of letters and other objects through a sliding panel at the back, and regularly used for the purpose by Madame Blavatsky or her agents.

"3. That there is consequently a very strong general presumption that all the marvellous narratives put forward in evidence of the existence of Mahatmas are to be explained as due either (*a*) to deliberate deception carried out by or at the instigation of Madame Blavatsky, or (*b*) to spontaneous illusion or hallucination or unconscious misrepresentation or invention on the part of the witnesses."

The mysterious appearances of the ghostly Mahatmas at the headquarters was shown, by Mr. Hodgson, to be the work of confederates, the cleverest among them being Madame Coulomb. Sliding panels, secret doors, and many disguises were the *modus operandi* of the occult phenomena. In regard to the letters and alleged precipitated writing, Mr. Hodgson says:

"It has been alleged, indeed, that when Madame Blavatsky was at Madras, instantaneous replies to mental queries had been found in the shrine (at Adyar), that envelopes containing questions were returned absolutely intact to the senders, and that when they were opened replies were found within in the handwriting of a Mahatma. After numerous inquiries, I found that in all cases I could hear of, the mental query was such as might easily have been anticipated by Madame Blavatsky; indeed, the query was whether the questioner would meet with success in his endeavor to become a pupil of the Mahatma, and the answer was frequently of the indefinite and oracular sort. In some cases the envelope inserted in the Shrine was one which had been previously sent to headquarters for that purpose, so that the envelope might have been opened and the answer written therein before it was placed in the Shrine at all. Where sufficient care was taken in the preparation of the inquiry, either no specific answer was given or the answer was delayed."

A certain phenomenon, frequently mentioned by Theosophists as having occurred in Madame Blavatsky's sitting-room, was the dropping of a letter from the ceiling, supposed to be a communication from some Mahatma. In all such cases conjuring was proved to have been used—the *deus ex machina* being either a silk thread or else a cunningly secreted trap door hidden between the wooden beams of the bungalow ceiling, operated of course by a concealed confederate.

Madam Blavatsky's favorite method of impressing people with her occult powers was the almost immediate reception of letters from distant countries, in response to questions asked. These feats were the result of carefully contrived plans, preconcerted weeks in advance. She would telegraph in cipher to one of her numerous correspondents, East Indian, for example, to write a letter in reply to a certain query, and post it at a particular date. Then she would calculate the arrival of the letter, often to a nicety. Her ability as a conversationalist enabled her to adroitly lead people into asking questions that would tally with the Mahatma messages. But sometimes she failed, and a ludicrous fiasco was the result. Mr. Hodgson's report contains accounts of many such mystic letters that would arrive by post from India in the nick of time, or too late for use.

Among other remarkable things reported of the Madame was her power of producing photographs of people far away by a sort of spiritual photography, involving no other mechanical process than the slipping of a sheet of paper between the leaves of her blotting pad.

When stories of this spirit-photography were rife

in London, a scientist published the following explanation of a method of making such Mahatma portraits:

"Has the English public never heard of 'Magic photography?' Just a few years ago small sheets of white paper were offered for sale which on being covered with damp blotting paper developed an image as if by magic. The white sheets of paper seemed blanks. Really, however, they were photographs, not containing gold, which had been bleached by immersing them in a solution of mercuric chloride. The latter gives up part of its chlorine, and this chlorine bleaches the brown silver particles of which the photograph consists, by changing them to chloride of silver. The mercuric chloride becomes mercurous chloride. This body is white, and therefore invisible on white paper. Now, several substances will color this white mercurous chloride black. Ammonia and hypo-sulphite of soda will do this. In the magic photographs before mentioned the blotting paper contained hypo-sulphite of soda. Consequently when the alleged blank sheets of white note paper were placed between the sheets of blotting paper and slightly moistened, the hypo-sulphite of soda in the blotting paper acted chemically on the mercurous chloride in the white note paper, and the picture appeared. As this was known in 1840 to Herschel, Blavatsky's miracle is nothing but a commonplace conjuring experiment."

3. Madame Blavatsky's Confession,

The individual to whom the world is most indebted for a critical analysis of Madame Blavatsky's character and her claims as a producer of occult phenomena is Vsevolod S. Solovyoff, a Russian journalist and *littcrateur* of considerable note. He has ruthlessly torn the veil from the Priestess of Isis in a remarkable book of revelations, entitled, "A Modern Priestess of Isis." In May, 1884, he was in Paris, engaged in studying occult literature, and was preparing to write a treatise on "the rare, but in my opinion, real manifestations of the imperfectly investigated spiritual powers of man." One day he read in the *Matin* that Madame Blavatsky had arrived in Paris, and he determined to meet her. Thanks to a friend in St. Petersburg, he obtained a letter of introduction to the famous Theosophist, and called on her a few days later, at her residence in the Rue Notre Dame des

Champs. His pen picture of the interview is graphic:

"I found myself in a long, mean street on the left bank of the Seine, *de l'autre cote de l'eau,* as the Parisians say. The coachman stopped at the number I had told him. The house was unsightly enough to look at, and at the door there was not a single carriage.

"'My dear sir, you have let her slip; she has left Paris,' I said to myself with vexation.

"In answer to my inquiry the concierge showed me the way. I climbed a very, very dark staircase, rang, and a slovenly figure in an Oriental turban admitted me into a tiny dark lobby.

"To my question, whether Madame Blavatsky would receive me, the slovenly figure replied with an *'Entrez, monsieur,'* and vanished with my card, while I was left to wait in a small low room, poorly and insufficiently furnished.

"I had not long to wait. The door opened, and she was before me; a rather tall woman, though she produced the impression of being short, on account of her unusual stoutness. Her great head seemed all the greater from her thick and very bright hair, touched with a scarcely perceptible gray, and very slightly frizzed, by nature and not by art, as I subsequently convinced myself.

"At the first moment her plain, old earthy-colored face struck me as repulsive; but she fixed on me the gaze of her great, rolling, pale blue eyes, and in these wonderful eyes, with their hidden power, all the rest was forgotten.

"I remarked, however, that she was very strangely dressed, in a sort of black sacque, and that all the fingers of her small, soft, and as it were boneless hands, with their slender points and long nails, were covered with great jewelled rings."

Madame Blavatsky received Solovyoff kindly, and they became excellent friends. She urged him to join the Theosophical Society, and he expressed himself as favorably impressed with the purposes of the organization. During the interview she produced her astral bell "phenomenon." She excused herself to attend to some domestic duty, and on her return to the sitting-room, the phenomenon took place. Says Solovyoff: "She made a sort of flourish with her hand. raised it upwards and suddenly, I heard distinctly, quite distinctly, somewhere above our heads, near the ceiling, a very melodious sound like a little silver bell or an Acolian harp.

"'What is the meaning of this?' I asked.

"'This means only that my master is here, although you and I cannot see him. He tells me that I may trust you, and am to do for you whatever I can. *Vous etes sous sa protection*, henceforth and forever.'

"She looked me straight in the eyes, and caressed me with her glance and her kindly smile."

This Mahatmic phenomenon ought to have absolutely convinced Solovyoff, but it did not. He asked himself the question:

"'Why was the sound of the silver bell not heard at once, but only after she had left the room and come back again?'"

A few days after this event, the Russian journalist was regularly enrolled as a member of the Theosophical Society, and began to study Madame Blavatsky instead of Oriental literature and occultism. He was introduced to Colonel Olcott, who showed him the turban that had been left at the New York headquarters by the astral Koot Hoomi. Solovyoff witnessed other "phenomena" in the presence of Madame Blavatsky, which did not impress him very favorably.

Finally, the High Priestess produced her *chef d'
œuvre*, the psychometric reading of a letter. Solovyoff
was rather impressed with this feat and sent an account of it to the *Rebus*, but subsequently came to
the conclusion that trickery had entered into it. When
the Coulomb exposures came, he did not see much of
Madame Blavatsky. She was overwhelmed with letters and spent a considerable time anxiously travelling
to and fro on Theosophical affairs. In August, 1885,
she was at Wurzburg sick at heart and in body, attended by a diminutive Hindoo servant, Bavaji by
name. She begged Solovyoff to visit her, promising
to give him lessons in occultism. With a determination to investigate the "phenomena," he went to the
Bavarian watering place, and one morning called on
Madame Blavatsky. He found her seated in a great
arm chair:

"At the opposite end of the table stood the dwarfish
Bavaji, with a confused look in his dulled eyes. He
was evidently incapable of meeting my gaze, and the
fact certainly did not escape me. In front of Bavaji
on the table were scattered several sheets of clean
paper. Nothing of the sort had occurred before, so

my attention was the more aroused. In his hand was a great thick pencil. I began to have ideas.

"'Just look at the unfortunate man,' said Helena Petrovna suddenly, turning to me. 'He does not look himself at all; he drives me to distraction'. . . Then she passed from Bavaji to the London Society for Psychical Research, and again tried to persuade me about the 'master.' Bavaji stood like a statue; he could take no part in our conversation, as he did not know a word of Russian.

"'But such incredulity as to the evidence of your own eyes, such obstinate infidelity as yours, is simply unpardonable. In fact, it is wicked!' exclaimed Helena Petrovna.

"I was walking about the room at the time, and did not take my eyes off Bavaji. I saw that he was keeping his eyes wide open, with a sort of contortion of his whole body, while his hand, armed with a great pencil, was carefully tracing some letters on a sheet of paper.

"'Look; what is the matter with him?' exclaimed Madame Blavatsky.

"'Nothing particular,' I answered; 'he is writing in Russian.'

"I saw her whole face grow purple. She began to stir in her chair, with an obvious desire to get up and take the paper from him. But with her swollen and almost inflexible limbs, she could not do so with any speed. I made haste to seize the paper and saw on it a beautifully *drawn* Russian phrase.

"Bavaji was to have written, in the Russian language with which he was not acquainted: 'Blessed are they that believe, as said the Great Adept.' He had learned his task well, and remembered correctly the form of all the letters, but he had omitted two in the word 'believe.' [The effect was precisely the same as if in English he had omitted the first two and last two letters of the word.]

" 'Blessed are they that *lie*,' I read aloud, unable to control the laughter which shook me. 'That is the best thing I ever saw. Oh, Bavaji! you should have got your lesson up better for examination!'

"The tiny Hindoo hid his face in his hands and rushed out of the room; I heard his hysterical sobs in the distance. Madame Blavatsky sat with distorted features."

As will be seen from the above, the Hindoo servant was one of the Madame's Mahatmas, and was caught .

in the act of preparing a communication from a sage in the Himalayas, to Solovyoff.

"After this abortive phenomena," remarks the Russian journalist, "things marched faster, and I saw that I should soon be in a position to send very interesting additions to the report of the Psychical Society." . . "Every day when I came to see the Madame she used to try to do me a favor in the shape of some trifling 'phenomenon,' but she never succeeded. Thus one day her famous 'silver bell' was heard, when suddenly something fell beside her on the ground. I hurried to pick it up—and found in my hands a pretty little piece of silver, delicately worked and strangely shaped. Helena Petrovna changed countenance, and snatched the object from me. I coughed significantly, smiled and turned the conversation to indifferent matters."

On another occasion he was conversing with her about the "Theosophist," and "she mentioned the name of Subba Rao, a Hindoo, who had attained the highest degree of knowledge." She directed Mr. Solovyoff to open a drawer in her writing desk, and take from it a photograph of the adept.

"I opened the drawer," says Solovyoff, "found the photograph and handed it to her—together with a packet of Chinese envelopes (See Fig. · 34), such as I well knew; they were the same in which the 'elect' used to receive the letters of the Mahatmas Morya and Koot Hoomi by 'astral post.'

" 'Look at that, Helena Petrovna! I should advise you to hide this packet of the master's envelopes farther off. You are so terribly absent-minded and careless.'

"It was easy to imagine what this was to her. I looked at her and was positively frightened; her face grew perfectly black. She tried in vain to speak; she could only writhe helplessly in her great arm-chair."

Solovyoff with great adroitness gradually drew from her a confession. "What is one to do," said Madame Blavatsky, plaintively, "when in order to rule men it is necessary to deceive them; almost invariably the more simple, the more silly, and the more gross the phenomenon, the more likely it is to succeed." The Priestess of Isis broke down completely and acknowledged that her phenomena were not genuine; the Koot Hoomi letters were written by herself and others in collusion with her; finally she exhibited to the journalist the apparatus for producing the "astral bell," and begged him to go into a co-partnership with her to astonish the world. He refused! The next day she declared that a black magician had spoken through her mouth, and not herself; she was not responsible for what she had said. After this he had other interviews with her; threats and promises; and lastly a most extraordinary letter, which was headed, "My Confession," and reads, in part, as follows:

"Believe me, *I have fallen because I have made up my mind to fall,* or else to bring about a reaction by telling all God's truth about myself, *but without mercy on my enemies.* On this I am firmly resolved, and from this day I shall begin to prepare myself in order to be ready. I will fly no more. Together with this letter, or a few hours later, I shall myself be in Paris, and then on to London. A Frenchman is ready, and a well-known journalist too, delighted to set about the work and to write at my dictation something short, but strong, and what is most important—a true history of my life. *I shall not even attempt to defend,* to justify myself. In this book I shall simply say: "In 1848, I, hating my husband, N. V. Blavatsky (it may have been wrong, but still such was the nature *God* gave me), left him, abandoned him—*a virgin.* (I shall produce documents and letters proving this, although he himself is not such a swine as to deny it.) I loved one man deeply, but still more I loved occult science, believing in magic, wizards, etc. I wandered with him here and there, in Asia, in America, and in Europe. I met with So-and-so. (You may call him a *wizard*, what does it matter to him?) In 1858 I was in London; there came out some story about a child, not mine (there will follow medical evidence, from the faculty of Paris, and it is for this that I am going to Paris). One thing and another was said of me; that I was depraved, possessed with a devil, etc.

"I shall tell everything as I think fit, everything I did, for the twenty years and more, that I laughed at the *qu'en dira-t-on*, and covered up all traces of what I was *really* occupied in, i. e., the *sciences occultes*, for the sake of my family and relations who would at that time have cursed me. I will tell how from my eighteenth year I tried to get people to talk about me, and say about me that this man and that was my lover, and *hundreds* of them. I will tell, too, a great deal of which no one ever dreamed, and *I will prove it*. Then I will inform the world how suddenly my eyes were opened to all the horror of my *moral suicide*; how I was sent to America to try my psychological capabilities; how I collected a society there, and began to expiate my faults, and attempted to make men better and to sacrifice myself for their regeneration. *I will name all* the Theosophists who were brought into the right way, drunkards and rakes, who became almost saints, especially in India, and those who enlisted as Theosophists, and continued their former life, as though they were doing the work (and there are many of them) and *yet were the first* to join the pack of hounds that were hunting me down, and to bite me .   .   .   .

"No!   The devils will save me in this last great hour. You did not calculate on the cool determination of *despair*, which *was* and has *passed over*. .   .   . And to this I have been brought by you.   You have been the last straw which has broken the camel's back under its intolerably heavy burden.   Now you are at liberty to conceal nothing.   Repeat to all Paris what you have ever heard or know about me.   I have already written a letter to Sinnett *forbidding him* to publish my *memoirs* at his own discretion.   I myself will publish them with all the truth.   .   .   . It will be a Saturnalia of the moral depravity of mankind, this *confession* of mine, a worthy epilogue of my stormy life.   .   Let the psychist gentlemen, and whosoever will, set on foot a new inquiry. Mohini and all the rest, even *India*, are dead for me. I thirst for one thing only, that the world may know all the reality, all the *truth*, and learn the lesson. And then *death*, kindest of all.   H. BLAVATSKY.

"You may print this letter if you will, even in Russia. It is all the same now."

This remarkable effusion may be the result of a fever-disordered brain, it may be, as she says, the "God's truth;" at any rate it bears the ear-marks of the Blavatsky style about it. The disciples of the High Priestess of Isis have bitterly denounced Solovyoff and the revelations contained in his book. They brand him as a coward for not having published his diatribe during the lifetime of the Madame, when she was able to defend herself. However that may be, Solovyoff's exposures tally very well with the mass of corroborative evidence adduced by Hodgson, Coues, Coleman, and a host of writers, who began their attacks during the earthly pilgrimage of the great Sibyl.

On receipt of this letter, Feb· 16, 1886, Solovyoff resigned from the Theosophical Society. He denounced the High Priestess to the Paris Theosophists, and the Blavatsky lodges in that city were disrupted in consequence of the exposures. This seems to be a convincing proof of the genuineness of his revelations. After the Solovyoff incident, Madame Blavatsky went into retirement for a while. Eventually she appeared in London as full of enthusiasm as ever and added to her list of converts the Countess of Caithness and Mrs. Annie Besant, the famous socialist and authoress.

Finally came the last act of this strange life-drama. That messenger of death, whom the mystical Persian singer, Omar Khayyam, calls "The Angel of the Darker Drink," held to her lips the inevitable chalice of Mortality; then the "golden cord was loosened and the silver bowl was broken," and she passed into the land of shadows. It was in London, May 8, 1891, that Helena Petrovna Blavatsky ended one of the strangest careers on record. She died calmly and peacefully in her bed, surrounded by her friends, and after her demise her body was cremated by her disciples, with occult rites and ceremonies. All that remained of her—a few handfuls of powdery white ashes—was gathered together, and divided into three equal parts. One portion was buried in London, one sent to New York

City, and the third to Adyar, near Madras, India. The New World, the Old World, and the still Older World of the East were honored with the ashes of H. P. B. Three civilizations, three heaps of ashes, three initials —mystic number from time immemorial, celebrated symbol of Divinity known to, and revered by, Cabalists, Gnostics, Rosicrucians, and Theosophists.

Mr. J. Ransom Bridges, who had considerable correspondence with the High Priestess from 1888 until her death, says (*Arena*, April, 1895): "Whatever may be the ultimate verdict upon the life and work of this woman, her place in history will be unique. There was a Titanic display of strength in everything she did. The storms that raged in her were cyclones. Those exposed to them often felt with Solovyoff that if there were holy and sage *Mahatmas*, they could not remain holy and sage, and have anything to do with Helena Petrovna Blavatsky. The 'confession' she wrote rings with the mingled curses and mad laughter of a crazy mariner scuttling his own ship. Yet she could be as tender and sympathetic as any mother. Her mastery of some natures seemed complete; and these people she worked like galley-slaves in the Theosophical tread mill of her propaganda movement.

"To these disciples she was the greatest thaumaturgist known to the world since the days of the Christ. The attacks upon her, the Coulomb and Solovyoff exposures, the continual newspaper calumnies they look upon as a gigantic conspiracy brewed by all the rules of the black art to counteract, and, if possible, to destroy the effect of her work and mission."

"Requiescat in Pace," O Priestess of Isis, until your next incarnation on Earth! The twentieth century will doubtless have need of your services! For the delectation of the curious let me add: the English resting place of Madame Blavatsky is designed after the model of an Oriental "dagoba," or tomb; the American shrine is a marble niche in the wall of the Theosophical headquarters, No. 144 Madison avenue, the ashes reposihg in a vase standing in the niche behind a hermetically-sealed glass window. The Oriental shrine in Adyar is a tomb modelled after the world-famous Taj Mahal, and is built of pink sandstone, surmounted by a small Benares copper spire.

4. The Writings of Madame Blavatsky.

Madame Blavatsky is known to the reading world as the writer of two voluminous works of a philosophical or mystical character, explanatory of the Esoteric Doctrine, viz., "Isis Unveiled," published in 1877, and the "Secret Doctrine," published in 1888. In the composition of these works she claimed that she was assisted by the Mahatmas who visited her apartments when she was asleep, and wrote portions of the manuscripts with their astral hands while their natural bodies reposed entranced in Thibetan Lamaseries. These fictions were fostered by prominent members of the Theosophical Society, and believed by many credulous persons. "Isis Unveiled" is a hodge-podge of absurdities, pseudo-science, mythology and folk-lore, arranged in helter-skelter fashion, with an utter disregard of logical sequence. The fact was that Madame Blavatsky had a very imperfect knowledge of English, and this may account for the strange mistakes in which the volume abounds, despite the aid of the ghostly Mahatmas. William Emmette Coleman, of San Francisco, has made an exhaustive analysis of the Madame's writings, and declares that "Isis," and the "Secret Doctrine" are full of plagiarisms. In "Isis" he discovered "some 2,000 passages copied from other books without proper credit." Speaking of the "Secret Doctrine," the master key to the wisdom of the ages, he says: "The 'Secret Doctrine' is ostensibly based upon certain stanzas, claimed to have been translated by Madame Blavatsky from the 'Book of Dzyan' —the oldest book in the world, written in a language unknown to philology. The 'Book of Dzyan' was the work of Madame Blavatsky—a compilation, in her own language, from a variety of sources, embracing the general principles of the doctrines and dogmas taught in the 'Secret Doctrine.' I find in this 'oldest book in the world' statements copied from nineteenth century books, and in the usual blundering manner of Madame Blavatsky. Letters and other writings of the adepts are found in the 'Secret Doctrine.' In these Mahatmic productions I have traced various plagiarized passages from Wilson's 'Vishnu Purana,' and Winchell's 'World Life'—of like character to those in Madame Blavatsky's acknowledged writings. * * * A specimen of the wholesale plagiarisms in this book appears in vol. II., pp. 599-603. Nearly the whole of four pages was copied from Oliver's 'Pythagorean Triangle,' while only a few lines were credited to that work."

Those who are interested in Coleman's exposé are referred to Appendix C, of Solovyoff's book, "A Modern Priestess of Isis." The title of this appendix is "The Sources of Madame Blavatsky's Writings." Mr. Coleman is at present engaged in the preparation of an elaborate work on the subject, which will in addition contain an "exposé of Theosophy as a whole." It will no doubt prove of interest to students of occultism.

5. Life and Death of a Famous Theosophist.

The funeral of Baron de Palm, conducted according to Theosophical rites, is an interesting chapter in the history of the Society, and worth relating.

Joseph Henry Louis Charles, Baron de Palm, Grand Cross Commander of the Sovereign Order of the Holy Sepulchre at Jerusalem, and knight of various orders, was born at Augsburg, May 10, 1809. He came to the United States rather late in life, drifted West without any settled occupation, and lived from hand to mouth in various Western cities. Finally he located in New York City, broken in health and spirit. He was a man of considerable culture and interested to a greater or less extent in the phenomena of modern Spiritualism. A letter of introduction from the editor of the *Religio-Philosophical Journal*, of Chicago, made him acquainted with Col. Olcott, who introduced him to prominent members of the Theosophical Society. He was elected a member of the Society, eventually becoming a member of the Council. In the year 1875 he died, leaving behind an earnest request that Col. Olcott "should perform the last offices in a fashion that would illustrate the Eastern notions of death and immortality."* He also left directions that his body should be cremated. A great deal of excitement was caused over this affair. in orthodox religious circles, and public curiosity was aroused to the highest pitch. The funeral service was, as Madame Blavatsky described it in a letter to a European correspondent, "pagan, almost antique pagan." The ceremony was held in the great hall of the Masonic Temple, corner of Twenty-third and Sixth avenue. Tickets of admission were issued of decidedly occult shape —*triangular;* some black, printed in silver; others drab, printed in black. A crowd of 2,000 people assembled to witness the obsequies. On the stage was a triangular altar, with a symbolical fire burning upon it. The coffin stood near by, covered with the orders of knighthood of the deceased. A splendid choir ren-

---

* "Old Diary Leaves"—*Olcott.*

dered several Orphic hymns composed for the occasion, with organ accompaniment, and Col. Olcott, as Hierophant, made an invocation or *mantram* "to the Soul of the World whose breath gives and withdraws the form of everything." Death is always solemn, and no subject for levity, yet I must not leave out of this chronicle the unique burlesque programme of Baron de Palm's funeral, published by the *New York World*, the day before the event. Says the *World:*

"The procession will move in the following order:

"Col. Olcott as high priest, wearing a leopard skin and carrying a roll of papyrus (brown card board).

"Mr. Cobb, as sacred scribe, with style and tablet.

"Egyptian mummy-case, borne upon a sledge drawn by four oxen. (Also a slave bearing a pot of lubricating oil.)

"Madame Blavatsky as chief mourner and also bearer of the sistrum. (She will wear a long linen garment extending to the feet, and a girdle about the waist.)

"Colored boy carrying three Abyssinian geese (Philadelphia chickens) to place upon the bier.

"Vice-President Felt, with the eye of Osiris painted

on his left breast, and carrying an asp (bought at a toy store on Eighth avenue.)

"Dr. Pancoast, singing an ancient Theban dirge:

> "'Isis and Nepthys, beginning and end :
> One more victim to Amenti we send.
> Pay we the fare, and let us not tarry.
> Cross the Styx by the Roosevelt street ferry.'"

"Slaves in mourning gowns, carrying the offerings and libations, to consist of early potatoes, asparagus, roast beef, French pan-cakes, bock-beer, and New Jersey cider.

"Treasurer Newton, as chief of the musicians, playing the double pipe.

"Other musicians performing on eight-stringed harps, tom-toms, etc.

"Boys carrying a large lotus (sunflower).

"Librarian Fassit, who will alternate with music by repeating the lines beginning:

> "'Here Horus comes, I see the boat.
> Friends, stay your flowing tears ;
> The soul of man goes through a goat
> In just 3,000 years.'

"At the temple the ceremony will be short and simple. The oxen will be left standing on the sidewalk, with a boy near by to prevent them goring the passers-by. Besides the Theurgic hymn, printed above in full, the Coptic National anthem will be sung, translated and adapted to the occasion as follows:

> "Sitting Cynocephalus up in a tree,
> I see you, and you see me.
> River full of crocodile, see his long snout !
> Hoist up the shadoof and pull him right out."

6. The Mantle of Madame Blavatsky.

After Madame Blavatsky's death, Mrs. Annie Besant assumed the leadership of the Theosophical Society, and wore upon her finger a ring that belonged to the High Priestess: a ring with a green stone flecked with veins of blood red, upon the surface of which was engraved the interlaced triangles within a circle, with the Indian motto, *Sat* (Life), the symbol of Theosophy. It was given to Madame Blavatsky by her Indian teacher. says Mrs. Besant, and is very magnetic. The High Priestess on her deathbed presented the mystic signet to her successor, and left her in addition many valuable books and manuscripts. The Theosophical Society now numbers its adherents by the thousands and has its lodges scattered over the United States, France, England and India. At the World's Columbian Exposition it was well represented in the Great Parliament of Religions, by Annie Besant, William Q. Judge, of the American branch,

FIG. 58. PORTRAIT OF MRS. ANNIE BESANT.

and Prof. Chakravatir, a High Caste Brahmin of
India.

Mrs. Besant, in an interview published in the *New
York World*, Dec. 11, 1892, made the following statement concerning Madame Blavatsky's peculiar
powers:

"One time she was trying to explain to me the control of the mind over certain currents in the ether
about us, and to illustrate she made some little taps
come on my own head. They were accompanied by
the sensation one experiences on touching an electric
battery. I have frequently seen her draw things to
her simply by her will, without touching them. Indeed, she would often check herself when strangers
were about. It was natural for her, when she wanted
a book that was on the table, to simply draw it to her
by her power of mind, as it would be for you to reach
out your hand to pick it up. And so, as I say, she
often had to check herself, for she was decidedly ad-
verse to making a show of her power. In fact, that is
contrary to the law of the brotherhood to which she
belonged. This law forbids them to make use of their
power except as an instruction to their pupils or as an
aid to the spreading of the truth. An adept may

never use his knowledge for his personal advantage. He may be starving, and despite his ability to materialize banquets he may not supply himself with a crust of bread. This is what is meant in the Gospel when it says: 'He saved others, Himself He cannot save.'

"One time she had written an article and as usual she gave me her manuscript to look over.

"Sometimes she wrote very good grammatic English and again she wrote very slovenly English. So she always had me go over her manuscript. In reading this particular one I found a long quotation of some twenty or thirty lines. When I finished it I went to her and said: 'Where in the world did you get that quotation?'

" 'I got it from an Indian newspaper of —,' naming the date.

" 'But,' I said, 'that paper cannot be in this country yet! How did you get hold of it?'

" 'Oh, I got it, dear,' she said, with a little laugh; 'that's enough.'

"Of course I understood then. When the time came for the paper to arrive, I thought I would verify her quotation, so I asked her for the name, the date of the issue and the page on which the quotation would be found. She told me, giving me, we will say, 45 as the number of the page. I went to the agent, looked up the paper and there was no such quotation on page 45. Then I remembered that things seen in the astral light are reversed, so I turned the number around, looked on page 54 and there was the quotation. When I went home I told her that it was all right, but that she had given me the wrong page.

" 'Very likely,' she said. 'Someone came in just as I was finishing it, and I may have forgotten to reverse the number.'

"You see, anything seen in the astral light is reversed, as if you saw it in a mirror, while anything seen clairvoyantly is straight."

The elevation of Mrs. Besant to the High Priestess-ship of the Theosophical Society was in accord with the spirit of the age—an acknowledgment of the Eternal Feminine; but it did not bring repose to the organization. William Q. Judge, of the American branch, began dabbling, it is claimed, in Mahatma messages on his own account, and charges were made against him by Mrs. Besant. A bitter warfare was waged in Theosophical journals, and finally the American branch of the general society seceded, and organized itself into the American Theosophical Society. Judge was made life-president and held the post until his death, in New York City, March 21st, 1896. His body was cremated and the ashes sealed in an urn, which was deposited in the Society's rooms, No. 144 Madison avenue.

Five weeks after the death of Judge, the Theosophical Society held its annual conclave in New York City, and elected E. T. Hargrove as the presiding genius of esoteric wisdom in the United States. It was originally intended to hold this convention in Chicago, but the change was made for a peculiar reason. As the press reported the circumstance, "it was the result of a request by a mysterious adept whose existence had been unsuspected, and who made known his wish in a communication to the executive committée." It seems that the Theosophical Society is composed of two bodies, the exoteric and the esoteric. The first holds open meetings for the discussion of ethical and Theosophical subjects, and the second meets privately, being composed of a secret body of adepts, learned in occultism and possessing remarkable spiritual powers. The chief of the secret order is appointed by the Ma-

hatmas, on account, it is claimed, of his or her occult
development. Madame Blavatsky was the High
Priestess in this inner temple during her lifetime, and
was succeeded by Hierophant W. Q. Judge. When
Judge died, it seems there was no one thoroughly
qualified to take his place as the head of the esoteric
branch, until an examination was made of his papers.
Then came a surprise. Judge had named as his successor a certain obscure individual whom he claimed
to be a great adept, requesting that the name be kept
a profound secret for a specified time. In obedience
to this injunction, the Great Unknown was elected as
chief of the Inner Brother-and-Sisterhood. All of this
made interesting copy for the New York journalists,
and columns were printed about the affair. Another
surprise came when the convention of exoterics ("hys-
terics," as some of the papers called them) subscribed
$25,000 for the founding of an occult temple in this
country. But the greatest surprise of all was a Theosophical wedding. The De Palm funeral fades away
into utter insignificance beside this mystic marriage.
The contracting parties were Claude Falls Wright,
formerly secretary to Madame Blavatsky, and Mary
C. L. Leonard, daughter of Anna Byford Leonard,

one of the best known Theosophists in the West. The ceremony was performed at Aryan Hall, No. 144 Madison avenue, N. Y., in the presence of the occult body. Outsiders were not admitted. However, public curiosity was partly gratified by sundry crumbs of information thrown out by the Theosophical press bureau.

The young couple stood beneath a seven-pointed star, made of electric light globes, and plighted their troth amid clouds of odoriferous incense. Then followed weird chantings and music by an occult orchestra composed of violins and violoncellos. The unknown adept presided over the affair, as special envoy of the Mahatmas. He was enveloped from head to foot in a thick white veil, said the papers.

Mr. Wright and his bride-elect declared solemnly that they remembered many of their former incarnations; their marriage had really taken place in Egypt, 5,000 years ago in one of the mysterious temples of that strange country, and the ceremony had been performed by the priests of Isis. Yes, they remembered it all! It seemed but as yesterday! They recalled with vividness the scene: their march up the avenue of monoliths; the lotus flowers strewn in their path by rosy children; the intoxicating perfume of the incense, burned in bronze braziers by shaven-headed priests; the hieroglyphics, emblematical of life, death and resurrection, painted upon the temple walls; the Hierophant in his gorgeous vestments. Oh, what a dream of Old World splendor and beauty!

Before many months had passed, the awful secret of the Veiled Adept's identity was revealed. The Great Unknown turned out to be a *she* instead of a *he* adept —a certain Mrs. Katherine Alice Tingley, of New York City. The reporters began ringing the front door bell of the adept's house in the vain hope of obtaining an interview, but the newly-hatched Sphinx turned a deaf ear to their entreaties. The time was not yet ripe for revelations. Her friends, however, rushed into print, and told the most marvellous stories of her mediumship.

W. T. Stead, the English journalist and student of psychical research, reviewing the Theosophical convention and its outcome, says (*Borderland*, July, 1896, p. 306): "The Judgeite seceders from the Theosophical Society held their annual convention in New York, April 26th to 27th. They have elected a young man, Mr. Ernest T. Hargrove, as their president. A former spiritual medium and clairvoyant, by name Katherine Alice Tingley, who claims to have been bosom friends with H. P. B. 1200 years B. C., when both were incarnated in Egypt, is, however, the grand Panjandrum of the cause. Her first husband was a detective, her second is a clerk in the White Lead Company's office in Brooklyn.

"According to Mr. Hargrove she is—'The new adept; she was appointed by Mr. Judge, and we are going to sustain her, as we sustained him, for we know her important connection in Egypt, Mexico and Europe.'"

In the spring of 1896, Mrs. Tingley, accompanied by a number of prominent occultists, started on a crusade through the world to bring the truths of Theosophy to the toiling millions. The crusaders before their departure were presented with a purple silk banner, bearing the legend: "Truth, Light, Liberation for Discouraged Humanity." The *New York Herald* (Aug. 16, 1896) says of this crusade:

"When Mrs. Tingley and the other crusaders left this country nothing had been heard of the claim of the reincarnated Blavatsky. Now, however, this idea is boldly advanced in England by the American branch of the society there, and in America by Burcham Harding, the acting head of the society in this country. When Mr. Harding was seen at the Theosophical headquarters, he said:

" 'Yes, Mme. Blavatsky is reincarnated in Mrs. Tingley. She has not only been recognized by myself and other members of the American branch of the Theosophical Society, who knew H. P. B. in her former life, but the striking physical and facial resemblance has also been noted by members of the English branch.'

"But this recognition by the English members of the society does not seem to be as strong as Mr. Harding would seem to have it understood. In fact, there are a number of members of that branch who boldly declare that Mrs. Tingley is an impostor. One of them, within the last week, addressing the English members on the subject, claimed that Mme. Blavatsky had foreseen that such an impostor would arise. He said:

" 'When Mme. Blavatsky lived in her body among us, she declared to all her disciples that, in her next reincarnation, she would inhabit the body of an Eastern man, and she warned them to be on their guard against any assertion made by mediums or others that they were controlled by her. Whatever H. P. B. lacked, she never wanted emphasis, and no one who knew anything of the founder of the Theosophical Society was left in any doubt as to her views upon this question. She declared that if any persons, after her death, should claim that she was speaking through them, her friends might be quite sure that it was a lie. Imagine, then, the feelings of H. P. B.'s disciples on being presented with an American clairvoyant medium, in the shape of Mrs. Tingley, who is reported to claim that H. P. B. is reincarnated in her.'

"The American branch of the society is not at all disturbed by this charge of fraud by the English branch. In connection with it Mr. Harding says:

" 'It is true that the American branch of the Theosophical Society has seceded from the English branch, but as Mme. Blavatsky, the founder, was in reality an American, it can be understood why we consider ourselves the parent society.'

"Of the one letter which Mrs. Tingley has sent to America since the arrival of the crusaders, the English Theosophists are a unit in the expression of opinion that it illustrated, as did her speech in Queen's

Hall, merely 'unmeaning platitudes and prophecies.'
But the American members are quite as loud in their
expressions that the English members are trying to
win the sympathies of the public, and that the words
are really understood by the initiate.

"The letter reads: 'In thanking you for the many
kind letters addressed to me as Katherine Tingley, as
well as by other names that would not be understood
by the general public, I should like to say a few words
as to the future and its possibilities. Many of you are
destined to take an active part in the work that the
future will make manifest, and it is well to press on-
ward with a clear knowledge of the path to be trodden
and with a clear vision of the goal to be reached.

" 'The path to be trodden is both exterior and interior, and in order to reach the goal it is necessary to
tread these paths with strength, courage, faith and the
essence of them all, which is wisdom.

" 'For these two paths, which fundamentally are
one, like every duality in nature, are winding paths,
and now lead through sunlight, then through deepest
shade. During the last few years the large majority
of students have been rounding a curve in the paths
of both inner and outer work. and this wearied many.

But those who persevered and faltered not will soon reap their reward.

" 'The present is pregnant with the promise of the near future, and that future is brighter than could be

FIG. 39. PORTRAIT OF MRS. TINGLEY.
[Reproduced by courtesy of the *New York Herald.*]

believed by those who have so recently been immersed in the shadows that are inevitable in cyclic progress. Can words describe it? I think not. But if you will

think of the past twenty years of ploughing and sow-
ing and will keep in your mind the tremendous
force that has been scattered broadcast throughout
the world, you must surely see that the hour for reap-
ing is near at hand, if it has not already come."

The invasion of English territory by the American
crusaders was resented by the British Theosophists.
The advocates of universal brotherhood waged bitter
warfare against each other in the newspapers and
periodicals. It gradually resolved itself into a struggle for supremacy between the two rival claimants for
the mantle of Madame Blavatsky, Mrs. Annie Besant
and Mrs. Tingley. Each Pythoness ascended her sacred tripod and hysterically denounced the other as an
usurper, and false prophetess. Annie Besant sought
to disprove the idea of Madame Blavatsky having
re-incarnated herself in the body of Mrs. Tingley. She
claimed that the late High Priestess had taken up her
earthly pilgrimage again in the person of a little Hindoo
boy, who lived somewhere on the banks of the Ganges.
The puzzling problem was this: If Mrs. Tingley was
Mme. Blavatsky, where was Mrs. Tingley? Oedipus
would have gone mad trying to solve this Sphinx
riddle.

The crusade finished, Mrs. Tingley, with her purple banner returned to New York, where she was royally welcomed by her followers. In the wake of the American adept came the irrepressible Annie Besant, accompanied by a sister Theosophist, the Countess Constance Wachmeister. Mrs. Besant, garbed in a white linen robe of Hindoo pattern, lectured on occult subjects to crowded houses in the principal cities of the East and West. In the numerous interviews accorded her by the press, she ridiculed the Blavatsky-Tingley re-incarnation theory. By kind permission of the *New York Herald*, I reproduce a portrait of Mrs. Tingley. The reader will find it interesting to compare this sketch with the photograph of Madame Blavatsky given in this book. He will notice at once how much the two occultists do resemble each other; both are grossly fat, puffy of face, with heavy-lidded eyes and rather thick lips.

7. The Theosophical Temple.

If all the dreams of the Theosophical Society are fulfilled we shall see, at no distant date, in the state of California, a sombre and mysterious building, fashioned after an Egyptian temple, its pillars covered with hieroglyphic symbols, and its ponderous pylons flanking the gloomy entrance. Twin obelisks will stand guard at the gateway and huge bronze sphinxes stare the tourist out of countenance. The Theosophical temple will be constructed "upon certain mysterious principles, and the numbers 7 and 13 will play a prominent part in connection with the dimensions of the rooms and the steps of the stairways." The Hierophants of occultism will assemble here, weird initiations like those described in Moore's "Epicurean" will take place, and the doctrines of Hindoo pantheism will be expounded to the Faithful. The revival of the Egyptian mysteries seems to be one of the objects aimed at in the establishment of this mystical college. Just what the Egyptian Mysteries were is a mooted question among Egyptologists. But this does not bother the modern adept.

Mr. Burcham Harding, the leading exponent of Theosophy mentioned above, says that within the temple the neophyte will be brought face to face with his own soul. "By what means cannot be revealed; but I may say that the object of initiation will be to raise the consciousness of the pupil to a plane where he will see and know his own divine soul and consciously communicate with it. Once gained, this power is never lost. From this it can be seen that occultism is not so unreal as many think, and that the existence of soul is susceptible of actual demonstration. No one will be received into the mysteries until, by means of a long and severe probation, he has proved nobility of character. Only persons having Theosophical training will be eligible, but as any believer in brotherhood may become a Theosophist, all earnest truthseekers will have an opportunity of admission.

"The probation will be sufficiently severe to deter persons seeking to gratify curiosity from trying to enter. No trifler could stand the test. There will be a number of degrees. Extremely few will be able to enter the highest, as eligibility to it requires eradication of every human fault and weakness. Those strong enough to pass through this become adepts."

The Masonic Fraternity, with its 33d degree and its elaborate initiations, will have to look to its laurels, as soon as the Theosophical College of Mystery is in good running order. Everyone loves mysteries, especially when they are of the Egyptian kind. Cagliostro, the High Priest of Humbug, knew this when he evolved the Egyptian Rite of Masonry, in the eighteenth century. Speaking of Freemasonry, it is interesting to note the fact, as stated by Colonel Olcott in "Old Diary Leaves," that Madame Blavatsky and her coadjutors once seriously debated the question as to the advisability of engrafting the Theosophical Society on the Masonic fraternity, as a sort of higher degree,—Masonry representing the lesser mysteries, modern Theosophy the greater mysteries. But little encouragement was given to the Priestess of Isis by eminent Freemasons, for Masonry has always been the advocate of theistic doctrines, and opposed to the pantheistic cult. At another time, the leaders of Theosophy talked of imitating Masonry by having degrees, an elaborate ritual, etc.; also pass words, signs and grips, in order that "one *occult* brother might know another in the darkness as well as in the *astral* light." This, however, was abandoned. The founding of the Temple of Magic and Mystery in this country, with ceremonies of initiation, etc., seems to me to be a palingenesis of Mme. Blavatsky's ideas on the subject of occult Masonry.

8. Conclusions.

The temple of modern Theosophy, the foundation of which was laid by Madame Blavatsky, rests upon the truth of the Mahatma stories. Disbelieve these, and the entire structure falls to the ground like a house of cards. After the numerous exposures, recorded in the preceding chapters, it is difficult to place any reliance in the accounts of Mahatmic miracles. There may, or may not, be sages in the East, acquainted with spiritual laws of being, but that these masters, or adepts, used Madame Blavatsky as a medium to announce certain esoteric doctrines to the Western world, is exceedingly dubious.

The first work of any literary pretensions to call attention to Theosophy was Sinnett's "Esoteric Buddhism." Of that production, William Emmette Coleman says:

" 'Esoteric Buddhism,' by A. P. Sinnett, was based upon statements contained in letters received by Mr. Sinnett and Mr. A. O. Hume, through Madame Blavatsky, purporting to be written by the Mahatmas Koot Hoomi and Morya—principally the former. Mr. Richard Hodgson has kindly lent me a considerable number of the original letters of the Mahatmas that leading to the production of 'Esoteric Buddhism.' I find in them overwhelming evidence that all of them were written by Madame Blavatsky. In these letters are a

number of extracts from Buddhist Books, alleged to
be translations from the originals by the Mahatmic
writers themselves. These letters claim for the adepts
a knowledge of Sanskrit, Thibetan, Pali and Chinese.
I have traced to its source each quotation from the
Buddhist Scriptures in the letters, and they were all
copied from current English translations, including
even the notes and explanations of the English trans-
lators. They were principally copied from Beal's 'Ca-
tena of Buddhist Scriptures from the Chinese.' In
other places where the 'adept' is using his own language in explanation of Buddhistic terms and ideas,
I find that his presumed original language was copied
nearly word for word from Rhys Davids' 'Buddhism,'
and other books. I have traced every Buddhistic idea
in these letters and in 'Esoteric Buddhism,' and every
Buddhistic term, such as Devachan, Avitchi, etc., to
the books whence Helena Petrovna Blavatsky derived
them. Although said to be proficient in the knowledge of Thibetan and Sanskrit the words and terms in
these languages in the letters of the adepts were nearly
all used in a ludicrously erroneous and absurd manner.
The writer of those letters was an ignoramus in Sanskrit and Thibetan; and the mistakes and blunders in

them, in these languages, are in exact accordance with the known ignorance of Madame Blavatsky concerning these languages. 'Esoteric Buddhism,' like all of Madame Blavatsky's works, was based upon wholesale plagiarism and ignorance."

Madame Blavatsky never succeeded in penetrating into Thibet, in whose sacred "lamaseries" and temples

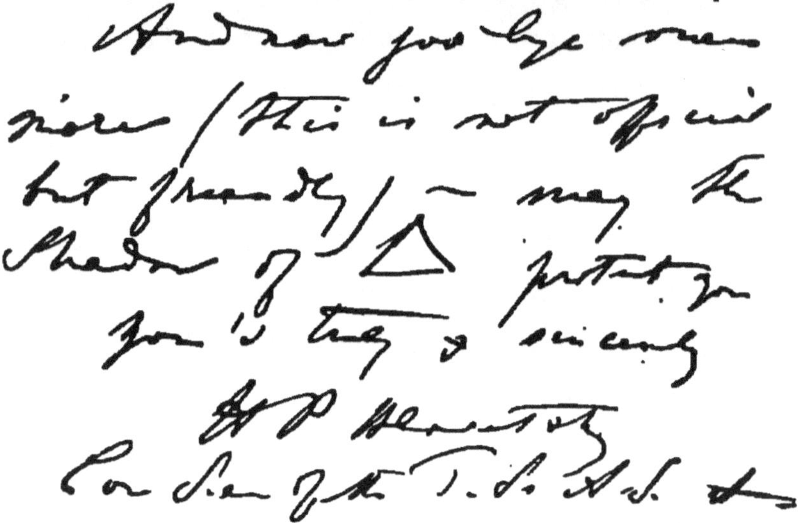

FIG 40. MADAME BLAVATSKY'S AUTOGRAPH.

dwell the wonderful Mahatmas of modern Theosophy, but William Woodville Rockhill, the American traveller and Oriental scholar, did, and we have a record of his adventures in "The Land of the Lamas," published in 1891. While at Serkok, he visited a famous monastery inhabited by 700 lamas. He says (page 102):

"They asked endless questions concerning the state of Buddhism in foreign lands. They were astonished that it no longer existed in India, and that the church of Ceylon was so like the ancient Buddhist one. When told of our esoteric Buddhists, the Mahatmas, and of the wonderful doctrines they claimed to have obtained from Thibet, they were immensely amused. They declared that though in ancient times there were, doubtless, saints and sages who could perform some of the miracles now claimed by the Esoterists, none were living at the present day; and they looked upon this new school as rankly heretical, and as something approaching an imposition on our credulity."

"Isis Unveiled," and the "Secret Doctrine," by Madame Blavatsky, are supposed to contain the completest exposition of Theosophy, or the inner spiritual meaning of the great religious cults of the world, but, as we have seen, they are full of plagiarisms and garbled statements, to say nothing of "spurious quotations from Buddhist sacred books, manufactured by the writer to embody her own peculiar views, under the fictitious guise of genuine Buddhism." This last quotation from Coleman strikes the keynote of the whole subject. Esoteric Buddhism is a product of Occidental manufacture, a figment of Madame Blavatsky's romantic imagination, and by no means represents the truth of Oriental philosophy.

As Max Mueller, one of the greatest living Oriental scholars, has repeatedly stated, any attempt to read into Oriental thought our Western science and philosophy or to reconcile them, is futile to a degree; the two schools are as opposite to each other, as the negative and positive poles of a magnet, Orientalism representing the former, Occidentalism, the latter. Oriental philosophy with its Indeterminate Being (or pure nothing as the Absolute) ends in the utter negation of everything and affords no clue to the secret of the Universe. If to believe that all is *maya*, (illusion), and that to be one with Brahma (absorbed like the rain drop in the ocean) constitutes the *summum bonum* of thinking, then there is no explanation of, or use for, evolution or progress of any kind. The effect of Hindoo philosophy has been stagnation, indifferentism, and, as a result, the Hindoo has no recorded history, no science, no art worthy the name. Compared to it see what Greek philosophy has done: it has transformed the Western world. Starting with Self-Determined Being, reason, self-activity, at the heart of the Universe, and the creation of individual souls by a process of evolution in time and space, and the unfolding of a splendid civilization are logical consequences. In the East, it is the destruction of self-hood; in the West the destruction of selfishness, and the preservation of self-hood.

Many noted Theosophists claim that modern Theosophy is not a religious cult, but simply an exposition of the esoteric, or inner spiritual meaning of the great religious teachers of the world. Let me quote what Solovyoff says on this point:

"The Theosophical Society shockingly deceived those who joined it as members, in reliance on the regulations. It gradually grew evident that it was no universal scientific brotherhood, to which the followers of all religions might with a clear conscience belong, but a group of persons who had begun to preach in their organ, *The Theosophist*, and in their other publications, a mixed religious doctrine. Finally, in the last years of Madame Blavatsky's life, even this doctrine gave place to a direct and open propaganda of the most orthodox exoteric Buddhism, under the motto of 'Our Lord Buddha,' combined with incessant attacks on Christianity. * * * Now, in 1893, as the direct effect of this cause, we see an entire religious movement, we see a prosperous and growing plantation of Buddhism in Western Europe."

As a last word let me add that if, in my opinion, modern Theosophy has no right to the high place it claims in the world of thought, it has performed its share in the noble fight against the crass materialism of our day, and, freed from the frauds that have too long darkened its poetical aspects, it may yet help to diffuse through the world the pure light of brotherly love and spiritual development.

LIST OF

Works Consulted in the Preparation of this Volume

AKSAKOFF, ALEXANDER N. **Animism and Spirit-ism**: an attempt at a critical investigation of mediumistic phenomena, with special reference to the hypotheses of hallucination and of the unconscious; an answer to Dr. E. von Hartmann's work, "Der Spiritismus." 2 vols. Leipsic, 1890. 8vo. (A profoundly interesting work by an impartial Russian savant. Judicial, critical and scientific.)

AZAM, DR. **Hypnotisme et Altérations de la Personnalité.** Paris, 1887. 8vo.

BERNHEIM, HIPPOLYTE. **Suggestive Therapeutics:** A study of the nature and use of hypnotism. Translated from the French. New York, 1889. 4to.

BINET, A., AND FÉRÉ, C. **Animal Magnetism.** Translated from the French. New York, 1888.

BLAVATSKY, MADAME HÉLÈNE PETROVNA HAHN-HAHN. **Isis Unveiled:** A Master-key to the mysteries of ancient and modern science and theology. 6th ed. New York, 1891. 2 vols. 8vo. (A heterogeneous mass of poorly digested quotations from writers living and dead, with running remarks by Mme. Blavatsky. A hodge-podge of magic, masonry, and Oriental witchcraft. Pseudo-scientific.)

—— **The Secret Doctrine:** The Synthesis of science, religion, and philosophy. 2 vols. New York, 1888. 8vo. (Philosophical in character. A reading of Western thought into Oriental religions and symbolisms. So-called quotations from the "Book of Dzyan," manufactured by the ingenious mind of the authoress.)

CROCQ FILS, DR. **L'hypnotisme.** Paris, 1896. 4to. (An exhaustive work on hypnotism in all its phases.)

CROOKES, WILLIAM. Researches in the Phenomena of Spiritualism. London, 1876. 8vo, (pamphlet).
—— Psychic Force and Modern Spiritualism. London, 1875. 8vo, (pamphlet). (Very interesting exposition of experiments made with D. D. Home, the spirit medium.)

DAVENPORT, R. B. Death Blow to Spiritualism: True story of the Fox sisters. New York, 1888. 8vo.

DESSOIR, MAX. The Psychology of Legerdemain. *Open Court*, vol. vii.

GARRETT, EDMUND. Isis Very Much Unveiled: Being the story of the great Mahatma hoax. London, 1895. 8vo.

GASPARIN, COMTE AGÉNOR DE. Des Tables Tournantes, du Surnaturel et des Esprits. Paris, 1854. 8vo.

GATCHELL, CHARLES. The methods of mind-readers. *Forum*, vol. xi, pp. 192-204.

GIBIER, Dr. PAUL. Le Spiritisme (fakirisme occidental). Étude historique, critique et expérimentale. Paris, 1889. 8vo.

GURNEY, E., MYERS, F W., AND PODMORE, F. Phantasms of the Living. 2 vols. London, 1887. (Embodies the investigations of the Society for Psychical Research into Spiritualism, Telepathy, Thought-transference, etc.)

HAMMOND, Dr. W. H. Spiritualism and Nervous Derangement. New York, 1876. 8vo.

HARDINGE-BRITTAN, EMMA. History of Spiritualism. New York. 4to.

HART, ERNEST. Hypnotism, Mesmerism and the New Witchcraft. London, 1893 8vo, (Scientific and critical, Anti-spiritualistic in character.)

HOME, D. D. Lights and Shadows of Spiritualism. New York, 1878. 8vo.

HUDSON, THOMAS JAY. The Law of Psychic Phenomena. New York, 1894. 8vo.
—— A Scientific Demonstration of the Future Life. Chicago, 1895. 8vo.

JAMES, WILLIAM. Psychology. New York, 1892. 8vo,
2 vols.

JASTROW, JOSEPH. Involuntary Movements. *Popular
Science Monthly*, vol. xl, pp. 743-750. (Interesting account
of experiments made in a Psychological Laboratory to demonstrate "the readiness with which normal individuals may
be made to yield evidence of unconscious and involuntary
processes." Throws considerable light on muscle-reading,
planchette-writing, etc.)

—— The Psychology of Deception. *Popular Science
Monthly*, vol. xxxiv, pp. 145-157.

—— The Psychology of Spiritualism. *Popular Science
Monthly*, vol. xxxiv, pp. 721-732.

(A series of articles of great value to students of psychical
research.)

KRAFFT-EBING, R. Experimental Study in the Domain of Hypnotism. New York, 1889.

LEAF, WALTER. A Modern Priestess of Isis; abridged
and translated on behalf of the Society for Psychical
Research, from the Russian of Vsevolod S. Solovyoff.
London, 1895. 8vo.

LILLIE, ARTHUR. Madame Blavatsky and her Theosophy. London, 1896. 8vo.

LIPPITT, F J. Physical-Proofs of Another Life: Letters
to the Seybert commission. Washington, D. C., 1888. 8vo.

MACAIRE, SID. Mind-Reading, or Muscle-Reading?
London, 1889.

MOLL, ALBERT. Hypnotism. New York, 1892. 8vo.

MATTISON, REV. H. Spirit-rapping Unveiled. An Exposé of the origin, history theology and philosophy of certain alleged communications from the spiritual world by
means of "spirit-rapping," "medium writing," "physical
demonstrations." etc. New York, 1855. 8vo.

MYERS, F W. H Science and a Future Life, and other
essays. London, 1891 8vo.

OCHOROWICZ, Dr. J. Mental Suggestion (with a preface by Prof. Charles Richet). From the French by J. Fitz-Gerald. New York, 1891. 8vo.

OLCOTT, HENRY S. Old Diary Leaves. New York, 1895. 8vo. (Full of wildly improbable incidents in the career of Madame Blavatsky. Valuable on account of its numerous quotations from American journals concerning the early history of the theosophical movement in the United States.)

PODMORE, FRANK S. Apparitions and Thought-Transference: Examination of the evidence of telepathy. New York, 1894. 8vo. (A thoughtful scientific work on a profoundly interesting subject.)

REVELATIONS OF A SPIRIT MEDIUM ; or, Spiritual-istic Mysteries Exposed. St. Paul, Minn., 1891. 8vo. (One of the best exposés of physical phenomena published.)

ROBERT-HOUDIN, J. E. The Secrets of Stage Con-juring. From the French, by Prof. Hoffmann. New York, 1881. 8vo. (A full account of the performances of the Davenport Bros. in Paris, by the most famous of con-temporary conjurers.)

ROARK, RURICK N. Psychology in Education. New York, 1895. 8vo.

ROCKHILL, WM. W. The Land of the Lamas. New York, 1891. 8vo.

SEYBERT COMMISSION ON SPIRITUALISM. Prelim-inary Report. New York, 1888. 8vo. (Absolutely anti-spiritualistic. The psychical phases of the subject not con-sidered.)

SIDGWICK, MRS. H. Article "Spiritualism" in "En-cyclopædia Britannica," vol. 22. (An excellent re-sumé of spiritualism, its history and phenomena.)

SINNETT, A. P. (*Ed.*) Incidents in the life of Mme. Blavatsky. London, 1886. 8vo. (Interesting, but replete with wildly improbable incidents, etc. Of little value as a life of the famous occultist.)

—— The Occult World. London, 1885. 8vo.

—— Esoteric Buddhism. London, 1888. 8vo.

SOCIETY FOR PSYCHICAL RESEARCH: Proceedings. Vols. 1-11. [1882-95.] London, 1882-95. 8vo. (The most exhaustive researches yet set on foot by impartial investigators. Scientific in character, and invaluable to the student. Psychical phases of spiritualism mostly dealt with.)

TRUESDELL, JOHN W. The Bottom Facts Concerning the Science of Spiritualism: Derived from careful investigations covering a period of twenty-five years. New York, 1883. 8vo. (Anti-spiritualistic. Exposés of physical phenomena : psychography, rope-tests, etc. Of its kind, a valuable contribution to the literature of the subject.)

WEATHERLY, Dr. L. A., AND MASKELYNE, J. N. The Supernatural. Bristol, Eng., 1891. 8vo.

WILLMANN, CARL. Moderne Wunder. Leipsic, 1892. 8vo. (Contains interesting accounts of Dr. Slade's Berlin and Leipsic experiences. It is written by a professional conjurer. Anti-spiritualistic.)

WOODBURY, WALTER E. Photographic Amusements. New York, 1896. 8vo. (Contains some interesting accounts of so-called spirit photography.)